"A HEART IS STOLEN"

The Marquis of Veryan awakes to find
himself, due to drink and desire, in a
strange bed. Beside him snoring and
looking unattractive, is Lady Rose
Caterham. Suddenly he remembers
that last night at a moment when he was
not in complete control of his
faculties, she had said: "You will
marry me, dearest Justin!"
Unfortunately he cannot remember his
reply, but he has the uncomfortable
feeling that it was in the affirmative.
The only possible course is for him to
escape and he and his friend Sir
Anthony Derville drive off before any
of his other guests are aroused, to one
of the Marquis's other houses which
he has not visited for five years. Here,
where he expected peace and quiet,
strange mysteries and intriguing
occurrences galvanise him into an
interest and excitement he has not
known before.
How he sets out to discover the truth
is told in this exciting, dramatic 259th
Book by Barbara Cartland.

OTHER BOOKS BY BARBARA CARTLAND

Barbara Cartland

A Heart Is Stolen

CORGI BOOKS
A DIVISION OF TRANSWORLD PUBLISHERS LTD

A HEART IS STOLEN

A CORGI BOOK o 552 11280 1

First publication in Great Britain

PRINTING HISTORY
Corgi edition published 1980

This book is set in Linotype Pilgrim

Corgi Books are published by
Transworld Publishers Ltd,
Century House, 61–63 Uxbridge Road,
Ealing, London W5 5SA
Set, printed and bound in Great Britain by
Cox & Wyman Ltd, Reading

ABOUT THE AUTHOR

Barbara Cartland, the world's most famous romantic novelist, who is also an historian, playwright, lecturer, political speaker and television personality, has now written over 250 books.

She has also had many historical works published and has written four autobiographies as well as the biographies of her mother and that of her brother, Ronald Cartland, who was the first Member of Parliament to be killed in the last war. This book has a preface by Sir Winston Churchill.

She has recently completed a very unusual book called "Barbara Cartland's Book of Useless Information", with a foreword by Admiral of the Fleet, the Earl Mountbatten of Burma. This is being sold for the United World Colleges of which he was President.

She has also sung an Album of Love Songs with the Royal Philharmonic Orchestra.

Barbara Cartland has to date, sold 100 million books over the world. In 1976 she broke the world record by writing twenty-one books, and her own record in 1977 with twenty-four.

In private life Barbara Cartland, who is a Dame of the Order of St. John of Jerusalem, Chairman of the St. John Council in Hertfordshire and Deputy President of the St John Ambulance Brigade, has also fought for better conditions and salaries for Midwives and Nurses. As President of the Royal College of Midwives (Hertfordshire Branch) she has been invested with the first Badge of Office ever given in Great Britain, which was subscribed to by the Midwives themselves. She has also championed the cause for old people, had the law altered regarding gypsies and founded the first Romany Gypsy camp in the world.

Barbara Cartland is deeply interested in Vitamin Therapy and is President of the British National Association for Health. She has a Health and Happiness Club in England and has just started one in America. Her book the Magic of Honey has sold over one million copies throughout the world and is translated into many languages.

AUTHOR'S NOTE

Ten days after Britain had signed peace with France in 1802, she began to disarm at an almost indecent speed. While Bonaparte continued to maintain vast armaments and to replenish his empty dockyards, Great Britain disbanded the Volunteers and halved her Army. Lord St. Vincent, the First Sea Lord used his immense prestige to secure drastic economies in Naval Administration, and within a few months 40,000 Sailors were discharged and hundreds of experienced officers relegated to half pay.

While every ship needed repairs after a long war, dockyard heads were dismissed, contracts with private Yards withdrawn and surplus stores sold – in some cases to French agents.

But such optimism was short-lived. On 18th May 1803 Britain was forced, once again, to declare war on France. Fortunately the war Napoleon had wanted and intended had come too soon. By forcing the issue before his Navy was ready, the English regained half the ground they had lost in the Peace.

All through the Centuries an Admiral took to sea his own servants, usually his valet, his Chef and his first footman, to wait on him at meals. He paid them himself. It was not until 1914 the Admiralty ordered that these servants should wear uniform and be put on the Naval payroll.

CHAPTER ONE

1802

The Marquis of Veryan woke and had the uncomfortable feeling he should not have been asleep.

Then he was aware that his head was throbbing and he had a dry bitterness in his mouth and remembered that last night he had imbibed too freely.

It was something that unlike his contemporaries, he seldom did, but it had been an extremely entertaining evening and his friends had been toasting his very successful season on the turf.

It was a toast to which he was obliged to reply and the wine, which he had chosen himself, had been exceptional.

Now he thought with almost a groan that he would have to pay for his enjoyment and was aware as he did so that he recognised the room in which he was lying, but it was not his own.

It was then that he heard a slight snore and turned his head – a movement which hurt him – to see that Rose was lying beside him and that she was still asleep.

He found himself looking at her, and something stirred in his memory but at the same time remained irritatingly elusive.

It was something she had said – what was it?

As he looked at her now he realised that she did not look her best, nor was her beauty at this moment at all 'goddess-like' which was the way he and every other man in the party had extolled it last night at dinner.

Now the mascara from her long eye-lashes had run onto

her cheeks and the crimson of her lips which had seemed irresistibly inviting had smudged onto her chin.

She snored again. It was only a very slight snore, but still a snore, and the Marquis turned his head from his contemplation of her to look up at the ruched satin of the four-poster over his head.

Now he remembered what he had been trying to recall and it came to him almost with the force of a thunder-bolt.

"You will marry me, dearest Justin?" Rose had said to him and he could not remember his reply.

He only knew that elated by the champagne and claret he had been drinking all the evening, and by the fact that she had surrendered after what had been not a long but definitely an arduous pursuit on his part, he was not responsible for whatever it was he had said.

Lady Rose Caterham had been the toast of St. James's and voted the 'Incomparable of Incomparables' among the Bucks and *Beaux* for the last two years.

Her husband had been killed in the war and as a widow she had dazzled the Social World which centred around the Prince of Wales. The prestige of her successive lovers had increased until finally she had caught the Marquis.

It had been no mean achievement; for while he was known to be the Protector of the most desirable and expensive 'Fashionable Impures', after remaining more or less faithful to the intelligent Lady Melbourne for many years, he had declared himself uninterested in the Social Beauties.

He thought the majority of them too pretentious and too artificial for his liking and found the frankness and the easy-going habits of ballet-dancers or women of the calibre of Harriet Wilson, much more to his taste.

Lady Rose had been determined to get the better of him and had used every allure and fascination in her repertoire, which was considerable, to entice and enslave the Marquis.

But she had been clever enough not to allow his conquest to be too easy.

She had given him 'a run for his money' as the Marquis

had described it to himself, and he had enjoyed the chase even while he knew the inevitable end only too well.

Perhaps he was being singularly obtuse but it had never actually struck him that Lady Rose wanted him not as a lover, but as a husband.

The idea of marrying her had never so much as entered his mind. In fact, marriage as far as he was concerned, was a subject so far removed from reality that he never discussed it except with his relatives.

Then it was only the older members of the family who took him to task for not providing an heir to inherit his vast possessions.

Now with a sense almost of horror he remembered Rose's lips seductively near to his saying:

"You will marry me, dearest Justin?" and he had no idea what he had answered.

He turned his head once again to look at her and knew as he did so, that the attraction she had had for him was over.

He had a sudden revulsion for her – a feeling which he had experienced before in his life and which he remembered had extremely unpleasant repercussions, involving tears, tantrums and scenes which he loathed and detested, but which never, however traumatic, forced him to change his mind.

"I am no longer interested in Lady Rose Caterham."

It was almost as if someone said the words aloud and they impinged sharply on his brain, telling him he had to do something about it.

Very, very gently, moving with the suppleness of a man whose body was trained to obey his will, the Marquis slipped out of bed.

Picking up his robe from where he had flung it on an adjacent chair, he walked with the stealth and quietness of a Red Indian across the thickly carpeted floor towards the door.

Then he glanced back at the bed to see if his departure had disturbed the sleeping woman.

13

To his relief she had not moved since he left her and again he could hear the slight snore, although now it was barely audible.

He managed to open the door without making any noise and stepping out into the passage he shut it again without a sound.

Then he hurried towards his own bedroom.

As he did so he looked down into the great marble Hall and realised that the light of the rising sun was shining at the sides of the curtains as it had done in Rose's bedroom, and he guessed from the strength of it, that it must be well after four o'clock.

There was only one tired footman in the carved and padded chair provided for those who had to endure the long hours of the night on duty.

The Marquis knew that at exactly five o'clock the household would be awake and the maid-servants and the underfootmen would swarm from the back premises to start cleaning and tidying the mess that he and his friends had made the night before.

There would be a large number of wine stained crystal glasses, some of them broken, empty decanters, wine-coolers in which the ice would have melted, and soft cushions which had been creased and thrown about.

Perhaps there would also be a satin slipper to be retrieved, a forgotten diamond ear-ring, and maybe even a crumpled cravat or two.

It was difficult for the Marquis to recall what actually had happened. He only knew it had been one of the rowdiest parties he had given for some time and now he regretted the fact that it had encroached on the dignity and beauty of his ancestral home.

He reached his bedroom more acutely conscious of his aching head than he had been before and decided what he needed was a cold bath.

His first action when he entered his bedroom, which was an extremely impressive chamber where his father and his grandfather had slept before him, was to jerk the bell which rang in his valet's room.

Then he pulled back the curtains to stand at the window looking out on the lake below him and beyond it at the Park with its ancient oak trees around which the early morning mist was swirling, looking almost like dancing nymphs.

The sky was translucent above the first radiance of the sun and there were still one or two wayward stars to be seen in the rapidly receding sable of the night.

It was time, the Marquis thought, when everything was silent and still and had a strange magical beauty that always stirred him with its promise of a new day.

Then he told himself sharply he had something more important to think about and that was Rose.

Now he was concentrating fiercely in an attempt to remember what he had replied to her plea that he should marry her.

Could he have been fool enough to have agreed to do so?

He was aware she had spoken when desire was burning through him like a flame and a man might say anything, and he could not help suspecting that she had chosen her moment well and carefully.

She had known exactly what she was about, while inflamed by her beauty and half-drugged by the wine he was not completely in control of his brain or himself.

"I could not have been so foolish – or could I?" the Marquis asked.

As he asked the question the door behind him opened and his valet came into the room.

"You rang, M'Lord?"

The valet spoke with no indication in his voice that there was anything unusual about being awoken so early, which was actually the truth.

He was a wiry little man who had been with the Marquis ever since he became old enough to have a valet, and who tended to him with a mixture of adoration and the protective severity of an anxious Nanny.

"Stop fussing over me, Hawkins," the Marquis would say time after time.

But he knew that Hawkins was essential to his comfort, and he too had an affection for the little man that was different from his feelings for any other servant he employed.

"I want a cold bath," he said now.

"I thought you might, M'Lord," Hawkins said laconically. "In fact I prepared it for you last night."

He opened a door leading off the bedroom into a small room which in the Marquis's father's time had been used as a powder-closet.

It contained a large bath which took an abnormal amount of hot water which had to be carried upstairs in brass cans by stalwart young footmen, but which was now three-quarters full of cold.

The valet glanced around the small room to see that a large, enveloping Turkish towel was laid over a chair, that the Marquis's soap and flannel were handy and the bath-mat emblazoned with the family crest was in its place. Then he said:

"Everything's ready for Your Lordship."

The Earl did not reply but merely pulled off his robe, handed it to Hawkins as he walked past him and got into the bath.

As he always took cold baths in the spring and summer it did not give him the shock it would have done to a softer living man.

His athletic body, which he kept slim from hours of riding obstreperous, often half-broken horses, was merely stimulated and invigorated by the water into which he also dipped his face and the whole of his head.

As he got out he already felt better, but the question as to what he should do about Lady Rose seemed more insistent.

Suddenly the words of his Commanding Officer when he first went into the Regiment came to him:

"Only a fool is not ready to retreat in the face of an overwhelming or unconquerable enemy. To do so, in certain circumstances, is not cowardice but commonsense."

"That is what I must do," the Marquis told himself, "retreat!"

Still rubbing himself dry with the towel he called through the open door:

"What is the hour, Hawkins?"

"Just on five o'clock, M'Lord."

"Go and wake Sir Anthony and tell him I want to speak to him."

"Very good, M'Lord."

As Hawkins went to obey his instructions the Marquis thought that if Anthony was not back in his room by this time, he should be.

He had obviously last night, been enamoured of a very pretty woman whose husband had unavoidably been prevented from joining the house-party.

The Marquis had wondered a little vaguely, because he was not really interested in anybody's love-affairs but his own, if it was not a possibility that Lord Bicester, who was notorious for cadging off his friends to pay his gambling debts, might be using Anthony, who was 'warm in the pocket' to bail him out.

It would not be the first time that his pretty wife had been useful in providing him with funds to continue gaming, although such an unpleasant and ominous word as 'blackmail' was never mentioned.

Then the Marquis thought that Anthony could look after himself. At the same time as it was his house and his party, he supposed he was in a way, responsible for what happened at it.

Anyway, he wanted simply to ask Anthony what his feelings were when he told him his own plans.

He threw his wet towel down on the floor and started to dress.

As Hawkins had obviously expected him to go riding, he had already laid out his exquisitely cut riding-clothes and a

17

pair of highly polished boots having the wide contrasting leather band at the top which had been introduced by Beau Brummel.

The Marquis had no wish to be a Dandy. At the same time like the Prince of Wales, he found Brummel's innovations on the social scene were all overdue.

Brummel's axioms on cleanliness, that a gentleman's linen must be spotless and changed twice a day, his decree that a coat must fit without a wrinkle and a cravat high and spotless, certainly improved every man's appearance.

The Marquis himself had always been fastidious as his father had been before him, but he realised that a great number of his acquaintances had been not only slovenly, but definitely dirty, and the change was certainly for the better.

He was dressed except for his cut-away coat with its long tails and was brushing his hair in front of the gold-framed mirror on the chest-of-drawers when his friend Sir Anthony Derville came into the room.

Anthony was tall and good-looking, and every woman thought he was one of the handsomest men she had ever seen until her eyes fell on the Marquis.

Together they were overwhelming and as one enraptured lady had exclaimed:

"It is just not fair for us wretched women to be offered not one ripe plum, but two, each as delectable as the other!"

"Why the devil did you have to wake me so early?" Sir Anthony demanded now as he crossed the room towards his friend. "I had only just got to sleep!"

"I have only just woken up," the Marquis replied.

He waited until Hawkins had shut the door behind his friend to wait outside in the corridor until he was wanted before he added:

"I am leaving, Anthony – are you coming with me?"

"Leaving? But why?"

The Marquis lowered his voice and told the truth.

"Rose proposed marriage last night and I cannot for the life of me remember what I said in reply."

"Good God!" Anthony ejaculated. "You must have been more 'foxed' than you appeared."

"She asked me when I was not in full possession of my faculties," the Marquis replied.

Anthony groaned.

"I always thought that Rose was up to snuff when it came to getting her own way."

"I am not going to marry her, if that is what you are inferring."

"So you are running away!"

"I prefer to call it a tactical withdrawal in the face of superior odds," the Marquis replied.

Then he smiled.

"Actually you are right, Anthony, I am not brave enough to stay and face the music. If she remembers what I promised last night, and I am quite certain she will, there will be a hell of a row if I make it quite clear I have no memory of what I said."

"Only what you did," Anthony remarked dryly.

The Marquis did not reply and after a moment he added:

"You might do worse than marry Rose. She is damned attractive!"

"Not early in the morning."

"So that is the rub! Well, it is best to find out before the ring is on the finger."

"There is going to be no ring on anybody's finger as far as I am concerned," the Marquis said sharply. "As you know, I have no wish to be married, and if I have to be shackled to some woman I can promise you it will not be to Rose Caterham."

"All right! All right!" his friend said. "There is no need to be truculent!"

"I feel truculent!" the Marquis said. "I know I made a fool of myself, but I have been in worse situations and got out of them."

Anthony threw back his head and laughed.

"Do you remember the time you shinned down a drain-pipe when the woman's husband returned unexpectedly? God, how I laughed when you told me about it! But it must have been pretty unpleasant at the time."

"It was!" the Marquis agreed briefly.

"Then there was that pretty little piece at Newmarket, what was her name?"

"Oh, for Heaven's sake, Anthony, stop reminiscing and go and get dressed, unless I am to go off alone."

"It will not take me long," Anthony said. "Tell Hawkins to arrange for one of the footmen to pack my things. I did not bring a valet as you know."

"Hawkins will see to it," the Marquis replied. "I will go and order breakfast."

"Brandy for me," Anthony said, "and I had better have coffee as well, if I am to keep awake."

He followed the Marquis towards the door.

"Where are we going?"

"I have not decided," the Marquis said, "but doubtless I will think of somewhere while we are eating."

"Well, for Heaven's sake, choose somewhere with comfortable beds," Anthony replied. "I shall need one by the time we reach our destination."

The Marquis did not reply because he was giving Hawkins instructions.

"Pack for me, Hawkins, and arrange for Sir Anthony's clothes to be ready when mine are. I will take my Phaeton and you can follow in the travelling chariot with Jem."

"Very good, M'Lord," Hawkins replied quite unperturbed at the sudden upheaval.

"Arrange to have Mr. Bradly awakened," the Marquis went on. "I will tell him what to do about the rest of the party after we have gone."

"I'll do that, M'Lord," Hawkins said. "Where are we going, if I might ask? So that I may know what clothes to pack for Your Lordship."

The Marquis put his hand up to his head as if it still ached.

"I have not really decided, Hawkins. What do you suggest?"

"I was only thinking yesterday, M'Lord, when Your Lordship remarked that it was unconscionably hot for September that I personally could do with a touch of the sea breezes, such as His Royal Highness must be enjoying at Brighton."

The Marquis stared at his valet and then gave an exclamation.

"You are right, Hawkins, of course you are right," he said. "We will go to Heathcliffe."

"A good idea, M'Lord. We've not been there for, let me see now, it must be four – or is it five – years?"

"It is five," the Marquis said, "although I drove there two years ago from Brighton for luncheon."

He stopped, then murmured beneath his breath:

"Heathcliffe will be the perfect place to hide."

Then in a louder voice he said:

"That is where we shall go, Hawkins, but keep the information entirely to yourself. I have no wish for my guests to follow me with the misguided idea that I need their company."

There was a knowing look in Hawkins' eyes as he said:

"I understand, M'Lord, but I think Your Lordship would be wise to send a groom ahead to alert them."

"I have always made it a rule that my houses, wherever they may be, are ready to receive me without notice," the Marquis said sharply.

"Of course, M'Lord," Hawkins said soothingly, "at the same time . . ."

"Oh, very well, have it your own way," the Marquis said. "I suppose you are thinking there will not be a decent meal ready for us if we do not give them notice of our arrival. But if everything else is not in order, I shall be extremely annoyed, make no mistake about that!"

Hawkins did not reply, he was hurrying down the corridor to carry out his instructions.

The Marquis as he walked slowly down the stairs, had a

feeling that it would be good for the servants at Heathcliffe to be awoken out of the lethargy into which they had doubtless succumbed after such a long absence on his part.

As it happened this was the second time he had thought of Heathcliffe in the last twenty-four hours.

Last night one of his guests Peregrine Percival, a somewhat dandified acquaintance he had not known for long, had offered him a pinch of snuff which was actually something he abhored.

"I never touch the stuff!" the Marquis had replied.

"Of course! I had forgotten!" was the reply. "but knowing your exceptional taste, I hope you admire my new snuff-box. I bought it only a few days ago."

The Marquis had taken the snuff-box in his hands and seen at once that it was not only valuable but unique.

It was not the diamonds that encircled it which interested him but the fact that in the centre, skilfully enamelled and ornamented with small gems, was a battleship.

It was depicted with billowing sails and rubies to portray the fire coming from its guns, while the sea was encrusted with very small emeralds.

The Marquis stared at it, then he said:

"I am sure I have seen this before."

"You have?" Peregrine Percival asked curiously. "I bought it from a Dealer, but he did not tell me to whom it had belonged."

"I remember now!" the Marquis exclaimed. "It must be the twin of one I actually own myself."

He saw the surprise in the face of the man listening and went on:

"My father collected a great many things which concerned the sea, for the house where he lived on the coast. The very replica of this box, unless I am mistaken, is among those he possessed."

"How interesting!" Peregrine Percival replied. "We must compare them sometime."

"Yes, we must do that," the Marquis agreed.

"I wonder what its history is. I imagine it was made some fifty or a hundred years ago."

"Quite that, I should think," the Marquis replied.

"It would be amusing to trace it, especially if we are both interested."

Then Rose had claimed the Marquis's attention and he had not thought of the snuff-box again.

Now the conversation came back to him and he thought that if he went to Heathcliffe he would certainly look for his snuff-box with the ship on it and see if his father had listed anything about it in the very accurate catalogue he had made of all his possessions which particularly interested him.

He suddenly thought how much he would enjoy being at Heathcliffe again. He had nearly forgotten, or rather it had not occurred to him for a long time, to think about the estate he owned on the South Coast.

The last three summers he had accompanied the Prince of Wales to Brighton because His Royal Highness specially requested his presence but three weeks had been enough to bore him with the same entertainments, the same gambling and meeting the same people night after night.

That happened again this year and he had left Brighton at the end of July to come to Veryan where he had been ever since.

There was a great deal to occupy him on his large estate in Kent where he owned ten thousand acres. He prided himself it was a model of its kind which definitely impressed everyone from the Prince himself downwards.

The Marquis entertained large house-parties and he had been training a number of horses with which he intended to win every important classic race for a great number of years to come.

It was not surprising that Heathcliffe, like his estate in Cornwall and another in the North, had not recently had the pleasure of his company, but he had received reports on them and had left what he believed to be able Agents in charge.

When he had time he went through the accounts of each establishment and made it his duty occasionally to query some particular item and ask for an explanation of it, just to keep those who represented him, up to scratch.

Heathcliffe was actually the smallest of his possessions, being less than five thousand acres in extent, a lot of it unfarmable.

His father had lived there the last years of his life, because the doctors considered the sunshine of the South was better for his health than the weather elsewhere in the British Isles.

It would have been even better for him had he been able to spend his time abroad, but first the French Revolution, then the war with Bonaparte had kept him in his native land.

Looking back now the Marquis remembered how much he had loved Heathcliffe when he was young, how he had enjoyed swimming in the sea and being able to feel freer there than in any of the other houses his father owned.

'Anthony and I will be on our own,' he thought, 'and that is what I want.'

He felt himself shudder as Rose's face with her smudged lips and running mascara appeared before his eyes.

Long before the guests at Veryan were awake the Marquis and Anthony were driving away in the Phaeton which had just been built for long-distance driving.

The family colours of blue and gold made it exceedingly smart, but it was doubtful if anyone after seeing the Marquis himself, would look at anything but the magnificent team of jet black horses which drew it.

They were perfectly matched and were the pride of the Marquis's stable as well as of their owner.

"Now do not take me too fast," Anthony admonished as they started down the drive. "My head feels as though it might crack open at any moment, and if you jerk me, I swear I shall fall to pieces at your feet!"

"You should have more self-control," the Marquis answered.

"I might say the same to you!" Anthony retorted. "What do you think your guests will say when they find you gone?"

"Personally, I have not the slightest interest in what they say," the Marquis replied. "I told Bradly to tell them I had been called away on important family business and that you had been kind enough to accompany me. If you ask me, I have done you a good turn in taking you away from Lucy Bicester."

"I am beginning to think that myself," Anthony said. "I had the uncomfortable feeling that Bicester might turn up last night unexpectedly, or that it was only a question of hours before she extracted out of me, some large sum I cannot afford."

There was silence as the team passed through the lodge-gates and the Marquis acknowledged the respectful curtsey of the woman who had opened them.

"It seems to me," Anthony said, "we have both had a lucky escape from situations which might prove disastrous to each of us!"

"If we have escaped!" the Marquis said beneath his breath.

"What can Rose do, even if she swears you promised to marry her?"

"I do not know, and I do not like to think about it," the Marquis replied. "I made it quite clear that nobody is to know where we have gone, so she should not be able to follow me."

"She will doubtless be waiting to pounce on you when we return to London."

"Oh, for God's sake, do not make it worse than it is already!" the Marquis said. "How could I have been such a fool as to not realise it was a wedding-ring she was after? I

25

was certainly not her first lover. Why should she want to marry me?"

Anthony laughed.

"Now, really, Justin, you sound like a surprised virgin! Of course she wanted to marry you rather than Leicester who has no money, or Selbirn who will have to wait at least another ten years before he comes into his father's title."

"You seem to know a lot about her."

"I watched Rose pursuing you," Anthony said, "and had the feeling that she might succeed in getting you on the hook."

"You could have taken the trouble to warn me."

"Warn you?" his friend exclaimed. "When have you ever allowed me to warn you about anything? You are always so certain you know best, and what is more, you would snap my head off, if I ever discussed your love-affairs."

This was so palpably true that the Marquis had nothing to say, but concentrated on driving his horses.

It was certainly some consolation to know that they moved perfectly in unison and were as smooth and easy to handle as any team he had ever known in the whole of his life.

"In future I shall keep to horses," he remarked.

Anthony laughed.

"Until the next Beauty sees you and is determined to get you into her clutches. The trouble with you, Justin, is that you are too handsome, too rich and too elusive."

'What do you mean by that?"

"I mean that women run after you because you make so little effort to run after them."

"The trouble is that I do not have to."

"That is what is wrong," Anthony said. "Women should appreciate that they are the prey, the final objective, and that is what makes the pursuit of them good fun."

"You had better tell that to Rose and your friend Lucy."

Anthony sighed.

"Stop being personal and let us try and talk objectively on the principle of the thing."

"What good will that do?" the Marquis enquired.

"It will clear our minds for the future," Anthony replied loftily. "Lucy has taught me a lesson, just as you have learned one from Rose Caterham. We would be fools not to profit by it."

"All right, I am listening to what you are trying to say," the Marquis said. "Come to the point."

"The point is that anything one gets too easily is not worth having. Agreed?"

"I suppose so."

"The women you and I know, let us face it, are extremely easy and bowled over quicker by you, than they are by me, because you have more to offer them. There is not a woman born who would not want to be the Marchioness of Veryan."

The Marquis did not reply but he was frowning, and Anthony knew that he was still apprehensive that he might find himself unavoidably married to Rose Caterham, and was aware how greatly he would dislike it.

As if the Marquis had spoken aloud, Anthony continued:

"Beauty is not enough; we both know that. Neither of us wants the type of wife who flirts with every man she meets and has not a thought in her head beyond being the belle of every Ball she attends."

There was silence for a moment until the Marquis said:

"Go on, Anthony, you are making sense and you are saying what I have always thought myself, but had not the brains to spell it out."

"My father used to say that every man should 'chew the cud'," Anthony went on, "and that is something you and I have often omitted to do, until it is too late and we have made quite a number of unnecessary mistakes."

"We do not want to go over that now," the Marquis said hastily, thinking of a number of incidents which were best forgotten.

"No, but you know what I am thinking about," Anthony went on. "Quite frankly, I believe we should be much more sensible in the future if we considered what we were doing before we did it."

"That is a gabbled sentence," the Marquis said critically, "but I get your meaning. The trouble is that we move in a very small circle and you and I, Anthony, do not exercise our brains by which we set so much score when we were at Oxford."

Seeing that the Marquis understood what he was trying to say, Anthony said:

"We are both in agreement."

The Marquis laughed.

"Of course!" he said, "but Heaven knows what the future may hold! I have the uncomfortable feeling that Rose and Lucy will quickly be replaced by two other 'Fair Charmers' of much the same calibre."

Anthony threw up his hands.

"Dammit all, Justin. You are as depressing as a wet race-meeting! Where is your sense of adventure? Your optimism, your faith in your guiding star?"

He spoke with an unmistakable mockery.

"Oh, shut up, Anthony!" the Marquis said. "Now you are depressing me and I am quite certain the only adventure we shall have on this trip will be a collision or a buckled wheel."

. . . .

The Marquis and Sir Anthony lingered so long over the luncheon they enjoyed at 'The Flying Fox' on the road, that they were later than they intended in reaching the coast.

As always, when they were alone together, they enjoyed their conversation, the jokes they made at each other's expense, and recalling incidents that had happened in the long years of their friendship.

Because they were both so exceptionally fit, the headaches from which they had been suffering when they awoke were dispersed over luncheon and they were both in excellent spirits as they set off on the last part of the drive.

With any other team the Marquis would have been obliged to change horses, but those he was driving had an Arab strain in them and he knew that if he took them fairly carefully over the last miles of the journey they would be able to stay the course.

"Now that peace has been declared," he said, "it is time for me to have my horses on the Dover Road again."

"I thought you might have done that already."

"I had not intended to go to France for another month," the Marquis explained. "I always think after a war, it is a good thing to let the country settle down and restore its more obvious comforts, before one pays it a visit."

"There are people already extolling the delights of Paris," Anthony replied, "and several men have told me they were agreeably impressed with their excellent reception from the moment they arrived at Calais. What is more, I am told the French women are fantastic!"

"We will go there next month," the Marquis promised. "Actually, Percival told me that in the Palais Royal the women all wear draperies in the Grecian mode with their hair anointed with scented oil."

Anthony laughed.

"We will certainly have to visit the Palais Royal and I would also like to see the First Consul. He cannot be quite such a monster as he is always depicted."

"I only hope he is not as clever as I suspect him to be," the Marquis remarked.

"What do you mean by that?"

"I have a suspicion that while we are wallowing in peace, forgetting old grievances and talking of the return of 'peace and plenty', Bonaparte might be taking advantage by building up his Army and his Fleet."

"Nonsense!" Anthony replied. "He is ready, just as we are, to let bygones be bygones."

"I hope you are right," the Marquis said. "But we will find out for ourselves when we get to France. Paris next month will be delightful, and certainly not as hot as it is now."

They talked of other things until ahead of them they saw the long line of the Downs and knew their journey was nearly at an end.

"It is years since I have been to Heathcliffe," Anthony said. "I remember staying with you when we were boys, and your father was in a terrible rage over something a neighbour had done to him."

"The Admiral, my father's arch-enemy!" the Marquis recalled. "The battle between those two old gentlemen had the blood coursing in their veins and their fury kept them young at heart until the very day my father died."

"What was the quarrel about?"

"I have forgotten – if I ever knew. When my father bought Heathcliffe, he found in the very centre of the estate only a mile from the house itself, there was a small Manor and ten acres belonging to a retired Admiral – what was his name?"

The Marquis paused before he said:

"Wadebridge! That was it! Admiral Horatio Wadebridge! He behaved as if he was still on the quarter deck, which made my father furious whenever he thought of him."

Anthony laughed.

"What did they fight about?"

"Everything, but mostly because the Admiral would not sell his home and estate to my father. There was no reason why he should but my father coveted 'Naboth's Vineyard', and he did everything in his power to gain possession of it without success."

"What has happened to the Admiral now?" Anthony asked.

"He must have died, like my father. They were both about the same age."

"And who now possesses Naboth's Vineyard, as you call it?"

"The Admiral had a son, so I suppose it belongs to him," the Marquis replied. "He is a good deal older than I am, so perhaps he has retired there waiting to quarrel with me when I need the sea air for my health."

"He will have to wait a long time," Anthony remarked. "On the other hand he might be willing to sell."

"Yes, I suppose he might," the Marquis agreed, "in which case I shall certainly buy the land."

"Have you not enough already?"

"I do not think one can ever have too much land," the Marquis replied. "Look at the Cecils – they have always added to their possession of land all through the centuries. I believe it is something I should do for those who follow after me."

"Good Heavens!" Anthony ejaculated. "You are planning ahead! Perhaps after all you should get married and continue the Veryan line who have done very well for themselves since Charles II."

"Charles I!" the Marquis corrected. "There are plenty of us – cousins by the score!"

"But you still want a son to carry on," Anthony persisted.

"Of course," the Marquis agreed, "but there is no hurry and let me make it quite clear – his mother's name will not be Rose!"

He spoke in such a ferocious tone that when Anthony laughed he had to join in.

Then the Marquis pointed with his whip.

"There is Heathcliffe!" he said. "Amongst those trees."

As he saw it, Anthony remembered the long low house which the Marquis's father had added to and improved with the help of one of the greatest architects of his time.

It was situated in a perfect position a little lower than the Downs, which rose behind it, and was sheltered in all sides except the front by a thick wood of trees which protected it from the winds which came in from the sea, and yet it gave the appearance of being majestically in command of the place on which it was situated.

For almost an hour they had been tasting the salt on the air and knowing a freshness that had been sadly lacking on the first part of their journey.

Now even the horses went a little quicker as if they were aware that they had reached their objective and a comfortable stable was waiting for them.

As they drove down the drive the house stood in front of them, built of red brick mellowed by the weather to a warm glowing pink, and Anthony said:

"I had forgotten that Heathcliffe was so beautiful. You should come here more often."

"That is exactly what I was thinking myself," the Marquis answered. "I cannot imagine why I have neglected it for so long."

"There is something very romantic about it," Anthony said reflectively. "Look at the flowers – they are breathtaking!"

"My father expended all his time and a great deal of his money on the garden," the Marquis said. "I was half-afraid that with the war and the shortage of man-power it might have become neglected, but I see my fears were groundless."

As they drew nearer to the house the evening sun glinted on its many windows seeming to glow with a warm welcome as they drove up to the front door.

Two grooms were waiting to go to the horses' heads, and as the Marquis stepped down feeling a little stiff after driving for so long, an elderly man with white hair appeared on the steps.

"Good-evening, Markham," the Marquis said.

"Good-evening, M'Lord, and may I welcome you home and say what a pleasure it is to have you here."

"Thank you, Markham," the Marquis replied. "I expect you remember Sir Anthony Derville from when he was a small boy?"

"I heard he was accompanying you, M'Lord, and it's a very great pleasure to see you again, Sir Anthony."

Mr. Markham who had been, the Marquis remembered,

his agent at Heathcliffe for over thirty years, led them into the cool Hall that was filled with flowers.

"I see you were expecting me?" the Marquis said.

"I was very grateful that Your Lordship was considerate enough to give me a few hours notice of your visit. Everything, as you are aware, is always in readiness, but there was time for the gardeners to bring in flowers and for warming pans to be placed in the beds which Mrs. Kingdom assured me is essential however carefully the sheets are aired."

The Marquis smiled, but did not reply as they walked into a long low room which overlooked the flower-garden at the back of the house.

It was the room in which his father had always sat in the evening and he almost expected him to rise from one of the comfortable arm-chairs and advance towards him.

Everything the late Marquis had collected was not only in perfect taste but also of great intrinsic value.

The Marquis looked around him with satisfaction, thinking the pictures on the walls which were all of ships, were very appropriate to the position of the house and that nothing had changed from when he was here as a boy.

"I anticipated Your Lordship would like a bath before dining," Mr. Markham said, "and it's already waiting for you upstairs, and a man who will look after you, until your own valet arrives."

"Hawkins will not be far behind, as we lingered rather longer than we intended over luncheon," the Marquis answered, "but the travelling-chariot could not be expected to keep up with my Phaeton."

He spoke with just a touch of pride in his voice and as if he knew this was a cue for congratulations, Mr. Markham said:

"I thought as Your Lordship was coming down the drive, I had never seen a finer team!"

'Neither have I, as it happens,' the Marquis agreed.

He turned to his friend.

"I expect, Anthony, you would like to wash off the dust before you do anything else?"

"I certainly would. At the same time, I would like a drink."

"There's a bottle of champagne cooling in the ice-bucket, M'Lord," Mr. Markham said, "and there's also some claret, should you prefer it.'

"Champagne for me," Anthony said, before the Marquis could reply, "and let us hope it is easier to obtain now we have peace."

"I do not suppose the people in this vicinity have had much difficulty in obtaining wine all through the war," the Marquis commented dryly. "Were our locals in the smuggling racket, Markham, like everybody else along the coast?"

"There's very little of it locally, M'Lord," Mr. Markham replied, "the big gangs, and I may say the dangerous ones, were all working near the Romney Marshes."

"I have heard a great deal about those particular smugglers," the Marquis said, "and I am relieved to hear you were not troubled by them. I am told they terrorised the local population."

"We were very fortunate, My Lord," Mr. Markham said.

He snapped his fingers at a servant who had followed them into the room and now at the signal, hurried to open the bottle of champagne.

The Marquis looked at him and saw he was a well built young man of about twenty-one or two.

He was wearing the Veryan livery but it did not seem to fit him very well, and the Marquis had the impression, but he was not certain why, that the man felt rather uncomfortable in it.

Then to his surprise, as the footman poured the champagne into the glasses, he saw that his wrist which just showed beneath the cuffs of his coat was tattooed.

"Were you in the Navy?" he enquired.

"Yes, M'Lord."

"Then I suppose you have only recently been discharged."

34

"Yes, M'Lord."

"That is interesting. I had imagined I would find only old servants in the house."

The footman looked quickly in the direction of Mr. Markham who explained:

"I'm afraid a number of the retainers you would remember, My Lord, either left us to go to the war, or retired through old age. We were able, recently, to fill their places with younger men like Billy here."

"That was lucky," the Marquis approved. "I hope Billy, you enjoy your new position."

"I be glad t'have it, M'Lord."

The Marquis was about to say something else but Anthony lifted his glass.

"Your health, Justin! And it is delightful to be back at Heathcliffe again!"

"Thank you," the Marquis said, "and Markham, you must have a glass too. Coming home is certainly an excuse for a celebration."

"That's very kind of you, My Lord."

He spoke in a tone that the Marquis thought was one of relief.

For a moment he wondered what his agent had to be relieved about, than as he drank the champagne, he forgot such an idea had even occurred to him.

CHAPTER TWO

The Earl came down early to dinner looking as resplendent in his evening-clothes as if he was going to a Reception at Carlton House.

As he descended the ancient oak staircase he noticed that the house smelt of bees'-wax and lavender and thought it was a vast improvement on the exotic perfumes which his women guests had used the night before.

He was in a mood when he was prepared to appreciate Heathcliffe and everything about it.

He was just going into the Drawing-Room when he thought he would first visit the Library, which had been his father's special Sanctum and where he had kept a great number of the treasures that had given him great pleasure because he had collected them personally.

The magnificent pictures at Veryan and at the family house in London had been inherited from the Marquis's grandfather who had a keen appreciation of art and had spent a great deal of time and money in assembling a collection which was spoken of as one of the best in the whole country.

He also had a good eye for furniture and had added to the superb pieces of red lacquer for which a Veryan in the reign of Queen Anne was responsible.

It had been difficult therefore for the late Marquis to improve on what he already possessed, but because he had excellent taste and a fortune which enabled him to indulge it, he had concentrated while he was at Heathcliffe, in buying antiques which had some connection with the sea.

The Marquis knew there were first editions of books on

the shelves of the Library which any connoisseur and certainly any Maritime Museum would love to possess.

All over the house were ship-pictures by famous artists that had made one of his fathers cronies declare that it was easier to feel sea-sick in Heathcliffe than in any ship he had ever boarded.

There was also his father's special collection of snuff-boxes.

These were each connected in some manner with the sea, and the Marquis remembered now that he wanted to look for the one which resembled the box belonging to Peregrine Percival, which he had inspected last night.

He thought it rather strange that there should be two boxes exactly the same, knowing most of the craftsmen of the period preferred to make something unique for their patrons.

At the same time he was aware that while one treasure, such as a Grecian vase, would be extremely valuable, if there was a pair they became not only worth four or five times as much, but in their own way, unique.

He opened the Library door and was aware that as in the Drawing-Room flowers had been arranged to herald his arrival.

He thought however, besides the fragrance of them, there was a slight smell of dust and ancient leather, and he walked across the room to open a window.

As he did so, he noted that all the things on his father's writing-table were arranged just as he remembered them – the blotter with its gold corners, embellished with the Veryan coat-of-arms, the large gold ink-stand, which had been made in the reign of Charles II by one of the greatest goldsmiths of his time, and all the other small objects in which his father had delighted.

There was a letter-opener set with precious gems, a magnifying glass, a pen-holder, a seal and a dozen other items which had thrilled the Marquis as a small boy.

He smiled as he looked at them. Then instinctively his

eyes went to where on the other side of the room was the large inlaid French cabinet with a glass top in which his father had kept his precious snuff-boxes.

"Now I will see," he said to himself, "if Peregrine Percival's box is any different from the one we possess."

He walked to the cabinet to stare into it with surprise, because there were far fewer snuff-boxes there than he had expected.

Had his memory been at fault? he asked.

He was sure in the past there had been so many that there was hardly room for more. Now lying on the dark blue velvet with which the cabinet was lined, there were a dozen boxes.

But they were arranged with gaps between them in a manner that might seem artistic, but made the Marquis feel that in some way, they were filling up space where there should have been others.

He made an effort to think back.

Surely he was not mistaken in thinking his father's collection was very much larger?

Perhaps some of them had been moved to another room, the Drawing-room, for instance?'

He looked down at what were already there and saw that most of them were distinctive and, he told himself, as far as he was concerned, unforgettable.

A number were ornamented with precious stones, but there was certainly not the ship in full sail on an emerald sea which he had recently been shown by Peregrine Percival.

Then it struck him that of course, Mr. Markham, being extremely zealous in his care of Heathcliffe, would have put away the most valuable snuff-boxes in the huge safe which he remembered stood in the Butler's Pantry.

That was where they would be, and the Marquis heaved a sigh of relief because for a moment he had been afraid that he had lost something which mattered to him because they had meant so much to his father.

"I must talk to Markham about it tomorrow," he told himself.

He knew there were a great number of things to discuss with his Agent, not only those which concerned the house, but also the estate.

He went from the Library back into the Drawing-Room to wait for Anthony.

As it was such a hot night the long French windows were open onto the terrace and he walked out to look down into the rose-garden and think how beautiful it was with the late roses still in bloom around an ancient sun-dial.

He could feel the faint breeze blowing in from the sea and he told himself he had been away from Heathcliffe far too long and another year he would definitely spend several weeks here.

Anthony came to join him.

"I cannot think why you have neglected this place, Justin," he said.

"It is what I was thinking myself," the Marquis replied, "and we will definitely come here next year instead of prancing up and down the Steine at Brighton talking to all those bores who have not an ounce of intelligence in their heads."

"Perhaps next year you will not invite me."

The Marquis looked at him in surprise and Anthony went on with a smile:

"I was thinking as I was dressing that this is the perfect place for a honeymoon."

"If you start talking about marriage all over again, I shall hit you,' the Marquis said. "We are here to preserve our bachelorhood, so let us drink on it."

He walked back into the Drawing-Room just as the footman came in carrying a tray on which there were two crystal glasses, accompanied by a Butler carrying a bottle of champagne wrapped in a napkin.

The Marquis looked at him and said:

"You are not Bateman!"

"No, M'Lord. My name's Travers."

"What has happened to Bateman?"

"He's retired, M'Lord. I believe he has a cottage in the village."

"I did not realise he was so old," the Marquis remarked. "I hope you will manage in his place and enjoy your duties at Heathcliffe."

"Thank you, M'Lord, I will endeavour to perform them to Your Lordship's satisfaction."

The Marquis liked the way the man spoke and it struck him he had a military bearing.

Then an idea came to him and he asked:

"Who were you with before Mr. Markham engaged you?"

"I was at sea, M'Lord."

The Marquis made no comment, but he looked at the man speculatively and decided that Markham had made a good choice.

It vaguely struck that now there was peace, there might be quite a number of Naval personnel looking for jobs.

He had however, always made it a rule on his estates that servants if possible should come from the families who had served him, his father before him, and often his grandfather.

At Veryan there were pantry-boys who represented the fifth generation and girls who considered it almost their right as soon as they were old enough, to be taken on at the 'big house'.

He had always imagined the same principle held good at Heathcliffe.

Then he tried to remember the size of the village which was situated over a mile and a half from the house and found it difficult to recall even approximately the number of inhabitants who lived there.

"You are very silent, Justin," Anthony remarked.

"I was thinking," the Marquis replied.

"I am so tired that I can think of nothing but how comfortable the bed in my room is likely to be."

"You are lucky you do not have to dance attendance on Lucy, and that is putting it politely."

"What do you bet Bicester turns up there tonight saying he has changed his mind and has decided to accept your invitation after all?"

"If he does, he will find an empty house," the Marquis replied. "You can be quite certain that Bradley will have bundled everyone back to London by now."

"I can imagine their fury!" Anthony said. "They were expecting to stay for at least another week."

"If you ask me house-parties always go on for far too long," the Marquis remarked. "For the first few nights the conversation seems witty and entertaining, but after that, one has heard all the jokes, and even one's drink seems to taste stale."

"You are spoilt, that is what is the matter with you!"

"Nonsense!" the Marquis replied. "We are just too intelligent for the type of people with whom we are forced to associate."

Anthony laughed.

"I would love to see their faces if they heard you say that!"

"For the moment I have no wish to see any of them again," the Marquis answered petulantly.

The Butler announced dinner and they walked into a delightful room which overlooked another part of the garden.

A huge window which almost covered one wall was open and the sun was sinking behind the trees in a blaze of glory.

"I wish I could paint that," the Marquis said.

"Van de Velde did his best," Anthony replied, "and I see you have two excellent pictures of his on the stairs."

"They portray the sea which is why my father bought them," the Marquis answered.

They sat down at the table which was lit by four candles in exquisitely chased gold candlesticks.

In the centre of them was a gold ship at which Anthony stared with undisguised admiration.

"I must say," he said, "I can well understand your father collecting everything to do with the sea. What I cannot understand is your taking so little interest in what he bought and leaving it here instead of taking it with you to Veryan or to London."

"I never thought of it," the Marquis said simply. "The things here belong to Heathcliffe and I like everything in its rightful place."

He thought again as he spoke, of the snuff-boxes and decided he would not show them to Anthony until they were all back in the show-case.

The dinner was good and the Marquis appreciated that the fish was fresh from the sea and the partridges, if a little tough, had obviously been shot when the household had been told of their arrival.

The beef however, was tender and excellent and Anthony who had a second helping of nearly everything, exclaimed when the fruit was put on the table:

"I have enjoyed my dinner! I had thought I was too tired to eat, but now I feel better."

"It is the sea air," the Marquis explained. "Wait until tomorrow. you will be ready to eat an ox all to yourself!"

"We shall need some exercise."

"A swim in the sea will provide that and of course, the horses. I have told Bradley to send us at least a dozen."

Anthony laughed.

"A grand gesture."

"I am determined you shall not be bored."

"I would be more impressed were I not certain you are really thinking of yourself!" Anthony teased.

"I have always found in the country one has to make one's own diversions," the Marquis said loftily, "and that is what I intend to do while we are hiding here."

"Hiding?" Anthony queried. "So you admit that is what you are doing?"

"Of course I am," the Marquis answered. "I do not intend

to return to London until I am quite certain there are no storms or tempests waiting for me."

"I have a feeling that might be a long time," Anthony smiled, "and knowing how easily you become bored, Justin, I am feeling rather apprehensive in case the peace and quiet of the country where nothing ever happens, palls too quickly."

"I will tell you if it does," the Marquis said, "but I know one thing – we shall find this brandy a considerable solace."

Anthony sipped from the glass which the servant had just put beside him.

"You are right," he said. "It is exceptional!"

"It must have been in the cellar a long time," the Marquis said, "or perhaps it crossed the Channel under the very nose of the coast-guards."

"Smugglers!" Anthony exclaimed. "Well, if you get really bored here we might even join them."

"There is no point in smuggling now the war is over," the Marquis said, "except to avoid paying the excise-men."

"No, that is true," Anthony agreed. "It seems to me the peace takes away quite a lot of the excitement in life except of course, where women are concerned."

"There you are, back on the same subject!" the Marquis exclaimed. "I refuse even to think of the Fair Sex or the dangers of smuggling, but will concentrate on peace and contentment."

"I will drink to that," Anthony said. "May your appreciation of such obvious virtues long continue!"

"The trouble with you is that you are a cynic!" the Marquis replied.

"That is the pot calling the kettle black!" Anthony exclaimed. "You have been one ever since I can remember. All I can say is if this mellow, benign mood lasts I shall be extremely surprised."

The Butler placed a decanter of port and one of brandy in front of the Marquis and he and the footmen withdrew from the Dining-Room.

There was the sound of a sudden crash outside which made the Marquis frown.

It had struck him over dinner that most of the waiting seemed to have been done by the Butler, while the four footmen seemed clumsy and ill at ease.

Their uniforms did not fit, and with his eye for detail and his desire for perfection, the Marquis decided this was another thing he must discuss with Markham tomorrow.

The sun was now only a golden glow on the horizon behind the trees, but they were still silhouetted against the changing sky.

There was the caw of the rooks going to roost in one of the big elms and the Marquis thought that he heard the first high squeak of a bat.

He leaned back in his chair and felt that he was, in fact, at peace with all the world.

Then suddenly there was a footstep at the window and a deep voice said:

"Do not move, gentlemen, please."

The Marquis stared in sheer astonishment.

Standing in the centre of the open window was a man with a pistol in each hand and he was wearing not a mask but a hood over his head which gave him a very strange appearance.

There were only slits for his eyes, his nose and his mouth, but beneath the hood he was conventionally dressed with a high, intricately tied white cravat, cut-away coat which fitted him to perfection, buckskin breeches and highly polished boots.

"What the devil . . .?" the Marquis began and would have moved but the man said again:

"Keep your place, My Lord, unless you wish to have a piece of lead blown through your shoulder."

The manner in which he spoke was quiet and slow, but there was also a note of determination which in its way was more menacing than if he had shouted.

Looking at the newcomer with fascinated eyes the

44

Marquis was aware that the door into the corridor had opened and he turned his head to see another man, also hooded, come into the room.

He held in his hand a black bag which appeared to be heavy and as he walked towards the table, the Marquis was aware that his clothes were very different from those of the man in the window.

They were the clothes of a servant and his coat was old-fashioned in shape and rather full.

He seemed to know exactly what to do, for he stood by the Marquis's side and the man in the window said:

"Kindly, gentlemen, place any money you have with you, on the table – also your jewellery."

The Marquis was calculating whether he would take a risk and whether, if he and Anthony charged the two men simultaneously they would prove too strong for the robbers.

Then, while he hesitated, through the door to the Servants' quarters came a third man.

He also carried a black bag in his hand.

Cursing at feeling so impotent, the Marquis pulled a purse from his pocket which contained quite a number of guineas because usually when they were alone together he and Anthony played piquet and it was easier to play for money than for I.O.U.s.

Anthony did the same.

"Your ring and your cravat-pin," the man in the window ordered.

Then to the Marquis, moving the pistol in this direction:

"I think My Lord, you are wearing a watch."

The Marquis stiffened, a refusal on his lips, but the pistol pointing at him from a distance of perhaps ten feet told him it would be foolish to take a risk.

The watch had been his father's and it was on a fob from which dangled a large, flawless emerald that he had always throught of as his 'luck'.

As it happened, he seldom wore the fob and never in the

45

day-time, because, like Beau Brummel, he thought that jewellery was ostentatious.

He had actually put it on tonight out of sheer sentiment. Now he was furious to think he had done so.

The hooded man beside him took the watch, the money, and the things which Anthony had placed on the table and waited for instructions.

"The ship in the centre of the table," the deep voice said. "Carry it carefully. It looks fragile and it would be a pity to spoil anything of such beauty."

There was no doubt they were being mocked and the Marquis felt a surge of sheer fury sweep over him, that made him clench his hands and tense his whole body, as if he might spring at the robber.

As if he knew what he was feeling, the man said:

"I should not do anything foolish, My Lord Marquis, an arm in a sling can be very restrictive."

Again there was that mocking note behind the words.

"Dammit!" the Marquis said, goaded at last into speech. "I will see that you hang on a gibbet, if it is the last thing I do."

"I doubt it," the Highwayman replied coolly. "But even that might give you a new interest, although not such an enjoyable one as winning a race or squiring a beautiful lady."

"I have no wish to listen to your impertinence," the Marquis retorted.

The Highwayman made a sound that was not exactly a laugh but more of a chuckle as if he was glad he had got under the Marquis's skin. Then he made a gesture with the pistol in his right hand and the two other men slipped past him through the window.

The Marquis heard them running across the garden.

The Highwayman waited, as if making sure they were safely away. Then he said:

"I suggest, Gentlemen, that you keep your seats for the next two minutes. If you are thinking of following me, I would like you to know that I am a very accurate shot."

As he spoke he moved back through the window still with his pistols pointed at the Marquis and Anthony.

Then with a swiftness that somehow seemed almost magical he vanished out of sight.

One moment he was there, the next he had gone and although the Marquis pushed back his chair and went to the open window, by the time he had reached it the garden, now in shadow, was quiet and empty.

Than as he listened, far away in the distance he heard the sound of galloping hoofs.

"My God, I would not have believed it!" Anthony exclaimed. "I have never been so astonished in my whole life!"

The Marquis was looking out into the garden still listening, then after a moment he said:

"I suppose it is useless to try and follow them?"

"I should imagine completely!" Anthony answered. "By the time we are mounted they could be two or three miles away."

They walked back to the table and sat down and the Marquis helped himself to a brandy and passed the decanter to his friend.

"Did you ever see anything so cool?" Anthony asked.

"This has been planned for a long time," the Marquis observed.

"Why should you think that?'

"Do you realise neither of the two men who were collecting the spoils, hesitated? They knew exactly what to do and waited only for the word of command."

"How the hell did they know we were here?" Anthony enquired. "After all, we only arrived unexpectedly this evening – unless they were intending to come anyway."

'It is a possibility,' the Marquis said. "At the same time, in that case why tonight?"

He looked at the space on the table where the gold ship had stood and said:

"I wonder what else they have taken?"

"We must go and look,' Anthony replied. "In the

meantime I need plenty of this brandy to sustain me. I am not used to Highwaymen walking in when I am having dinner."

"They were certainly different from any Highwaymen I have seen before," the Marquis said. "Why the hoods? Usually a mask or a handkerchief up to the eyes is sufficient."

"Yes, that is true," Anthony agreed. "Do you remember that one who held us up on Hampstead Common? You shot him in the leg. I can still hear his screams as he galloped away."

"I hardly expected I should have to be armed in my own Dining-Room," the Marquis said savagely.

"I have never heard of this happening to anyone else," Anthony remarked.

"It is not the sort of thing that ought to be happening at Heathcliffe," the Marquis said, "and if there are men like that terrorising the neighbourhood, then Markham should have warned us."

"I cannot believe that he would expect such a thing to happen the first night we arrive," Anthony said.

He put his hand up to where his cravat-pin had been and said angrily:

"I wish I had not broken my rule of never wearing jewellery. To tell the truth, I tied my own cravat and tied it so badly as I was tired, that I required a pin to keep it in place."

"The one thing I mind their taking," the Marquis said, "is my father's watch and my fob."

"We do not know what else they have taken."

The Marquis made a sound that was almost a cry.

"I bet it was the snuff-boxes," he said. "I was looking at them before dinner and I thought they were too valuable to leave lying about. I can only pray they did not get the ones in the safe."

As he spoke he remembered the third man who had come through the door which led towards the kitchen.

He jumped up and walked across the room, and opened the door which the Highwayman had shut behind him, went into the Pantry that adjoined the Dining-Room.

One look was enough to tell him his worst fears had been realised.

The door of the huge safe which almost covered one wall in the Pantry was open.

It was something he knew always happened when a dinner was in progress, the gold and silver ornaments had to be taken from the safe and placed on the table, then returned to it when dinner was over.

It would be too much to expect the servants to lock the safe for the short time that the meal was in progress.

The Marquis pulled the safe door wide seeing, as he spoke, inside it on the narrow shelves there were still a great number of items, tea-pots, coffee-jugs, gold candelabra which were used at big banquets, huge piles of silver plate that were kept for special dinners.

It was impossible to know whether the snuff-boxes had been there or not and he was aware that only Markham would be able to ascertain exactly what was missing.

Still extremely angry because he felt so helpless the Marquis without speaking walked from the Pantry and along the passage which led to the Hall.

There, followed by Anthony, he went into the Library.

Although it was dusk there were no candles lit in this room but it was quite easy to see in the faint light that came from the windows that the top of the glass cabinet was open.

The Marquis went through the motions of looking to see what was left inside, knowing the answer before he did so.

"Curse it!" he said furiously. "They have taken every one of my father's snuff-boxes!"

"I am sorry, Justin," Anthony said sympathetically.

"We ought to have done something – we ought to have stopped them."

"That is what I thought," Anthony agreed, "but quite

frankly I did not like the look of that fellow's pistols. I am quite prepared to believe he is the crack shot he boasted of being."

The Marquis with difficulty prevented himself from cursing the Highwayman with every oath he had ever learned in the Army. At the same time, his dignity told him there was no point in sinking to the level of the robbers, even if this one was different.

Later in the Drawing-Room they went over the man's points for future identification.

"I suppose you could say he was a gentleman," Anthony said. "He spoke like one."

'He had a peculiarly low voice which I would recognise again," the Marquis added.

"So should I," Anthony agreed. "He was not very tall, but very slim and athletic in the way he moved, and he was well dressed."

"Dammit, that might apply to hundreds of men," the Marquis said. "The only real clue we have to his identity is that his voice was deeper than most people's."

"I have thought of something else," Anthony remarked.

"What is that?"

"He must have known the layout of the house. While one of his men cleared the snuff-boxes out of the Library, the other must have moved into the Pantry almost as soon as the servants had left for their own supper. At least, I imagine that is what they were having."

The Marquis nodded.

"At Veryan they dine as soon as we have finished, and I know my Chef there always lets the footmen have what he calls the 'left-overs' which they appreciate."

"That proves my point," Anthony said. "They knew there would be nobody in the Pantry and they cleared out the snuff-boxes and timed to do so exactly as their chief walked in through the window, knowing that it would be open."

"You certainly have a point there," the Marquis agreed reflectively. "I will tell you something else."

"What is that?"

"As their horses were leaving they sounded fresh. I can always tell if a horse had been ridden a long way, because he sounds not exactly tired, but a little heavy. I would not mind betting those horses had not come far."

"That narrows the field considerably," Anthony said.

He yawned.

"Highwaymen, or no Highwaymen, unless they have taken my bed I want to go to sleep."

"Then that is what we shall do," the Marquis agreed. "There is no point in rousing the household tonight. It will mean hours of talk and speculation, and I do not suppose Markham can tell us any more than we can tell him."

"I could not stand it," Anthony yawned. "For God's sake let us leave it until tomorrow."

"We will do that," the Marquis agreed, "and now I think of it I am as tired as you must be."

At the same time, after he had told Hawkins what had happened as he helped him undress, it was a long time before he got to sleep.

. . . .

The next morning, immediately after breakfast the Marquis sent for his agent.

Markham had already been informed as to what had happened the night before, by other members of the household who had been regaled by Hawkins.

"I cannot believe it, M'Lord!" the elderly man said unhappily, wringing his hands in anguish. "The gold ship by which his late Lordship set so much store and the snuffboxes!"

"A very heavy loss where I am concerned," the Marquis said. "Had you any idea there were villains lurking in the neighbourhood?"

"No, My Lord, but of course we are very isolated here at Heathcliffe and sufficient, as you might say, unto ourselves."

"Who are our nearest neighbours?"

"There are not many, My Lord. Colonel Lloyd – you may remember him – died last year, and the house is now empty. Lord Moorland, who was a friend of His late Lordship's is bedridden, and has not left his home for a twelve-month."

"There are no other large houses of a similar sort with pickings such as these criminals found here?"

"No, My Lord."

The Marquis thought for a moment, then he asked:

"What about the Admiral?"

"Do you mean Admiral Wadebridge, My Lord?"

"Of course!"

"He has been dead for nigh on six years, My Lord."

"I thought he must be," the Earl remarked. "What about his son?"

"Your Lordship did not know that he was killed at the Battle of the Nile?"

"I had no idea. Although I suppose he was an hereditary enemy, considering the animosity between my father and the Admiral, I am sorry he should have lost his life."

"He was a fine man, My Lord, and with his death I believe the Navy lost a great Captain."

The Marquis looked at his agent sharply.

"You knew him?"

For a moment there was a pause as if Mr. Markham regretted the warm manner in which he had spoken. Then he said a little hesitatingly:

"Yes, My Lord. I knew Captain Wadebridge. It would be difficult to live here without doing so."

The Marquis smiled.

"I can understand, Markham, that you must find it very lonely here, but I suppose you have your own family?"

"Your Lordship must have forgotten that I am un-married."

"I am sorry, Markham, it had in fact slipped my memory," the Marquis apologised.

He wondered what his connection with Flagstaff Manor

might be and remembered how the Admiral had renamed his
house as a gesture of defiance to annoy his father.

Again Mr. Markham seemed to hesitate before he said:

"Captain Wadebridge's son, My Lord, is of course in the
Navy, but he is, I believe, in the West Indies at the moment."

"I seem to remember there was a girl," the Marquis said
frowning in an attempt at concentration.

"Yes, My Lord, that would be Miss Ivana."

"I never met the children at the Manor," the Marquis said,
"but she would have been younger than I. I imagine that
Ivana, if that is her name, must have grown up by now."

"I am sure Your Lordship is right," Mr. Markham said.
"Would Your Lordship wish me to inform the Magistrates of
what has occurred last night?"

The Marquis had the feeling he was deliberately changing
the subject and because he felt Mr. Markham had no wish to
answer any more questions, he asked:

"What does Miss Wadebridge do with herself all day? She
can hardly be living alone at the Manor, unless her mother is
alive."

"Mrs. Wadebridge died many years ago, My Lord."

"Then who else is at the Manor?"

"I really cannot say. Although I knew Captain Wadebridge, the two houses do not communicate."

There was a note in Mr. Markham's voice which told the
Marquis that for no reason he could ascertain, he was on the
defensive.

There must be something strange about the Wadebridges,
he thought, but then there always had been.

In the old days he had only to mention the name to have
his father roaring with anger at the iniquities of something
the Admiral had said or done. He was quite certain that the
Admiral did the same thing when he thought of the Marquis.

Later generations were surely too sensible to carry on a
feud which had kept the blood pulsating through two old
hearts and had given them an interest in life they would not
otherwise have had.

"I wonder," the Marquis said reflectively, "whether the Highwaymen who robbed Sir Anthony and me so successfully last night, also called on Miss Wadebridge? It would have been frightening for her if they did so. After all, if we could not compete with them, what could she do?"

"I feel, My Lord, it is extremely unlikely there would be anything in Flagstaff Manor to interest the type of criminal who came here."

"Why should you think that?" the Marquis asked.

"Surely it is obvious, My Lord. They knew what they wanted."

"They must also have known," the Marquis said, "that half the snuff-boxes had been removed from the Library into the safe."

Mr. Markham did not speak and the Marquis was aware that he was holding himself rather stiffly.

"I was going to speak to you about them today," he went on, "but I quite understand that you would have put them all in what you considered to be a safe place and only taken out a certain number before my arrival. Is that correct?"

"Yes, My Lord, completely correct," Mr. Markham replied.

The note of relief in his voice was very obvious.

The Marquis thought that his agent must have been afraid that he would be blamed for not having such valuable possessions as the snuff-boxes and the gold ornaments on the Dining-Room table, locked up while the servants were at supper.

'He is a very conscientious man,' the Marquis told himself.

He was rather touched that Markham should care so sincerely about the things he had guarded for so many years.

"I will of course, My Lord, make all possible enquiries as to whether anyone else has seen the Highwaymen," Mr. Markham was saying, "but I have the uncomfortable feeling, that we shall never hear of them again."

The Marquis did not contradict him. He had suddenly

made up his mind on a course of action and rose from the chair in which he had been sitting to say:

"Tell the grooms to bring two horses to the front door. Sir Anthony and I will go riding. Then later in the day, when it is really warm, we might swim in the sea as I used to when I was a boy."

"I am sure Your Lordship will enjoy that," Mr. Markham said. "I will send the order to the stables immediately."

He walked as far as the door, then he looked back to say:

"I can only say how deeply sorry I am, My Lord, that this unfortunate robbery should have occurred the first night on which you honoured us with your presence."

"Thank you, Markham."

As the agent left the room the Marquis turned almost eagerly to Anthony:

"We are going on a journey of exploration."

"To find what?" Anthony asked.

"The truth about several things which puzzle me."

"Are you fancying yourself as a sleuth?"

"As a matter of fact I am," the Marquis replied, "and I find it distinctly intriguing."

CHAPTER THREE

The Marquis and Sir Anthony walked into the Hall and as the Marquis took his tall hat from one of the footmen he saw that Mr. Markham was standing under the stairs.

"By the way, Markham," he said, "what is the name of young Wadebridge who I imagine, has now inherited the property?"

There was a pause before Mr. Markham said in a rather strange tone:

"His name is Charles, My Lord. Have you any reason for asking?"

"I thought it might seem unnatural if I am so ignorant about our nearest neighbours," the Marquis replied.

As he spoke, he was walking down the steps to where the horses were waiting and Anthony asked:

"Are you saying that we are going to call on Naboth's Vineyard? If so, I shall be interested to see it."

"So will I," the Marquis replied. "It has been forbidden ground ever since I can remember."

They were busily engaged in mounting their horses which were fresh, and once they were in the saddle and had set off Anthony said:

"I think we had better give our mounts their heads before we do anything else. I will race you across the Park."

"Right," the Marquis replied.

Setting his hat more firmly on his head they were off, turfs being thrown into the air behind them by the horses' hoofs.

In about a mile they drew in their reins and Anthony exclaimed:

"Dammit, Justin, I cannot think why you always have so much better horses than I can acquire. Would you like to sell the one I am riding?"

"Certainly not!" the Marquis replied. "You know I never sell my horses."

"I was not particularly hopeful when I asked," Anthony said with a grin.

They trotted for a little while until they reached a wood. Then the Marquis turned in the opposite direction.

"Now we will go a-calling," he said, "and I shall be interested to see what sort of reception we get."

"Feelings obviously run high in this part of the world." Anthony remarked. "I saw your agent's face when he re-alised where you were going. It was a macabre study in horror!"

The Marquis laughed.

"Poor old Markham! He remembers how ferociously and violently my father hated the Admiral, and I think servants always identify themselves with their masters' likes and dislikes."

They rode on and a little while later they saw in front of them a brick wall which the Marquis remembered encircled the Admiral's house.

It was not hard to find the entrance for just inside the gates there was an enormous flagstaff flying the White Ensign.

Anthony laughed.

"I am not surprised that annoyed your father."

"Even though he could not see it, he knew it was there," the Marquis said.

As they turned in at the gate the Marquis looked back the way they had come and saw in the distance a man riding between the trees on what struck him as a particularly well-bred horse.

He wondered vaguely if it was a neighbour whom Mark-ham had not mentioned, then he and Anthony were riding up a short drive which ended in an elegantly laid out garden in front of an ancient Elizabethan manor with gabled roofs and casement windows.

It was an extremely attractive house, but what struck the Marquis immediately was the extraordinarily precise tidiness of the garden.

The small flower-beds and the paths were all edged with stones which must have come from the beach and they had been painted white so as, he thought with amusement, to give them the neatness one might find aboard a ship.

As they reached the front door a man appeared to take their horses and one look at him told the Marquis he was obviously a Naval type.

He dismounted saying as he did so:

"Good-morning. Is Miss Wadebridge at home?"

"Oi thinks so, Sir," the man answered with an accent which the Marquis did not recognise but was certain did not belong to Sussex.

He walked to the front door and knocked on it with the butt of his riding-whip and even as Anthony joined him the door was opened by an elderly maid who dropped a respectful curtsey.

"I have called to see Miss Wadebridge," the Marquis said.

"Mrs. Wadebridge will be pleased to receive you, M'Lord," the maid replied. "Will you please come this way?"

She walked ahead of him and the Marquis thought in her neat grey dress she looked more like a child's Nanny than a servant and she reminded him of one he had had himself up to the age of seven.

The hall was small but attractively panelled and the oak staircase shone as if it had been subjected to a great deal of polishing.

The old maid opened a door and announced:

"The Marquis of Veryan, Ma'am, and friend."

The Marquis's first impression was of a very attractive room with two bow windows, bowls of flowers arranged beside a pretty fireplace and an atmosphere that he could only describe to himself as cosy and home-like.

A woman rose from a chair beside the fireplace and as he walked towards her, he thought that the Admiral's grandchild had certainly grown into a very attractive young woman.

She was dark, which surprised him because he had always imagined that people who had a lot to do with the sea were fair, but her eyes were blue with dark lashes, and he guessed she must have Irish blood in her.

She was very slim and her gown was old-fashioned, having a full skirt and a white fichu which had gone out of vogue at the end of the century.

Its colour was a deep emerald green which gave her skin a translucent whiteness, and she had what the Marquis realised with his experienced eye was exceptional beauty for a country-woman.

She curtsied and the Marquis bowed, then as her eyes looked into his, he realised to his surprise that she was frightened.

He told himself it was because she was shy and unused to meeting Gentlemen of Fashion, but her voice was calm and composed as she said:

"Good-morning, My Lord."

"Good-morning," the Marquis replied. "May I present my friend, Sir Anthony Derville?"

She curtsied again and Anthony, with a smile most women found irresistible said:

"This is the most attractive house I have seen in a long time, Mrs. Wadebridge. I can well understand why your grandfather was determined not to lose it."

There was an answering smile on the woman's lips as she replied:

"I see you have been told of the war that existed for so many years between the two estates."

"That is why I feel you must be surprised to see me," the Marquis said.

"It is of course a pleasant surprise, My Lord. Will you not sit down?"

59

She indicated with her hand a sofa on the other side of the fireplace and the Marquis seated himself with Anthony beside him.

"May I offer you some refreshment?"

"No, thank you," the Marquis replied. "We have not long had breakfast, but my friend and I thought we should call on you as early as possible, to discover if, by any unfortunate chance, you were a victim last night of the Highwaymen."

"Highwaymen?"

Her tone was one of sheer astonishment and the Marquis explained:

"We arrived at Heathcliffe yesterday evening and as it was a last-minute decision on my part to come here, nobody could have known in advance that was my intention."

Mrs. Wadebridge was listening to him attentively, her blue eyes with their long dark lashes fixed on his face.

"While we were dining," the Marquis continued, "a Highwayman wearing a hood, not a mask, and two other men with him, came into the Dining-Room."

Mrs. Wadebridge clasped her hands together.

"How could they have done that?"

"The window was open," the Marquis explained. "Their leader came in from the garden, but the two other men were already in the house."

"I can hardly believe it!"

"It is unfortunately true, and they left taking with them some irreplaceable treasures including the snuff-boxes which belonged to my father and were a unique collection."

"How terrible!" Mrs. Wadebridge exclaimed. "It must have been a great shock."

"It was," the Marquis answered, "even more so because Sir Anthony and I could do nothing to prevent the robbery as we were both unarmed, and it would have been extremely foolhardy to have attempted to fight three men who were."

"I understand how frustrated you must have felt," Mrs.

Wadebridge said. "Have you notified the Magistrates?"

"Not yet," the Marquis replied, "I thought I would first discover who else in the neighbourhood had seen this gang of criminals. But you tell me everything was quiet here."

"Yes, indeed, but I am very grateful you have warned me about them as there is only my old Nanny and myself in the house, and we should have been utterly at their mercy."

"I heard your brother Charles was at sea," the Marquis said, "but I was not told that you were married."

Mrs. Wadebridge looked down and he saw the colour rise in her cheeks.

"My husband is also a sailor, My Lord."

"And his name is the same as your own?"

"I married a distant cousin. There are quite a number of Wadebridges. It is, as Your Lordship is doubtless aware, a well known name in Naval circles."

"I must offer you my condolences on your father's death," the Marquis said. "The Battle of the Nile was a great victory."

"It was indeed," Mrs. Wadebridge agreed, "and Admiral Nelson is a great strategist."

There was a little pause. Then the Marquis said:

"I hope, Mrs. Wadebridge, that now after so many years, we have had the pleasure of meeting each other, we shall be able to behave as near neighbours in an ordinary, friendly fashion."

"I hope so too, My Lord," Mrs. Wadebridge replied. "Will you be staying long at Heathcliffe?"

The Marquis might have been unusually perceptive, but he had the feeling that she was anxious to hear the answer to her question.

He did not reply immediately and he was aware that she was looking at him enquiringly and almost as if whatever he said was of particular importance.

"I have not yet made up my mind," he answered at length. "Sir Anthony and I came here for peace and quiet."

"I cannot believe the Highwaymen will trouble you again, My Lord."

"I certainly hope not."

Again there was a pause and the Marquis had the idea he was expected to leave.

Because he was intrigued, he said:

"May I look at your garden? And perhaps the rest of the house. I admit to being extremely curious after so many years of being forbidden to cross your threshold."

Mrs. Wadebridge laughed.

"As I was forbidden to cross yours. I cannot tell you how tantalising it was to see Heathcliffe in the distance, to have glimpses of magnificent horses and fine coaches going up and down the drive and imagining the parties inside the house, to which I would never be invited."

"I can see that it must have been infuriating," the Marquis laughed.

'Being a woman, I think it made me more miserable than angry."

"Well, if you have never seen Heathcliffe, its owner will now be able to show it to you," Anthony said eagerly.

The Marquis glanced at him and realised he was looking at Mrs. Wadebridge with admiration and was aware that Anthony had not missed the fact that she was extremely pretty. In fact, the Marquis told himself, lovely was the right word.

As if he knew it was expected of him, with just a touch of amusement in his voice he said:

"I should, of course, be delighted to show you Heathcliffe and its contents, even if my father's snuff-boxes are no longer there."

"But there are lots of other things worth seeing," Anthony added, "especially the pictures."

He looked at the Marquis and asked deliberately:

"Why should not Mrs. Wadebridge dine with us one evening? We have, as it happens, not many engagements."

"Yes, of course," the Marquis agreed. "What evening would suit you?"

He looked at Mrs. Wadebridge as he spoke and had the idea she was considering the invitation before she replied to it.

It struck him as strange that she was not more eager, and because she was reluctant, he decided that it might be because of the old feud, and the sooner that was laid to rest the better.

Aloud he said:

"I think if you agree to dine with me, Mrs. Wadebridge, we could then be quite certain we had 'buried the hatchet' for all time. Would tomorrow night suit you? I will send a carriage to pick you up at half-after-seven."

"That is very kind of you, My Lord, and I shall be very pleased to dine at Heathcliffe."

The Marquis noted that she did not say: "to dine with you" but he supposed her choice of words was of no significance.

Surely she could not wish to identify herself after all these years with the childish animosity that had existed between two old men.

He rose to his feet.

'I shall look forward to showing you my house," he said, "and now may I see yours?"

He thought she hesitated, but was not sure. Then moving ahead of him she said:

"There is really not very much to see."

The Marquis and Sir Anthony followed her out into the hall and she showed them the Dining-room where the old oak furniture which matched the period of the house was polished like the stairs and the brass handles were so brilliant that they seemed to mirror everything around them.

She then took them into the Study, over the mantelpiece of which was a portrait of her grandfather in his Admiral's uniform and beneath it in a glass case a long row of his medals and decorations.

He looked a belligerent old man with a beard and had an aggressive air about him as if he was permanently on guard against the enemy.

"An excellent likeness," the Marquis said, "and when you see my grandfather you will see they were well paired."

"You certainly do not resemble him," Anthony said to Mrs. Wadebridge with a caressing note in his voice.

"I am told I take after my mother," Mrs. Wadebridge replied, "whose family came from Ireland."

"I was sure of it!" Anthony exclaimed, "blue eyes set in with dirty fingers!" That is very Irish!"

Mrs. Wadebridge laughed.

"So I am always told, but I have never been fortunate enough to visit the Emerald Isle."

She would have led the way from the study but the Marquis had walked to the window to look out at what he knew was the back of the house.

To his surprise he saw not a garden as he expected, but what was a court-yard and beyond it a huge and ancient barn.

"That seems a strange thing to have attached to the house," he said. "A tithe barn!"

Mrs. Wadebridge smiled.

"I see you are not aware, My Lord, that before your grandfather bought Heathcliffe, most of the estate was Wadebridge land."

"I had no idea!" the Marquis exclaimed.

"The Wadebridges who lived here for several hundred years were rich and important," Mrs. Wadebridge explained, "but over the centuries they spent so much time at sea that gradually they had to sell their possessions ashore."

"Now I can understand why you hated the Veryans," the Marquis said. "May I look at your barn a little nearer?"

Again Mrs. Wadebridge hesitated and he had the feeling that she was longing for them to leave.

Obstinately he determined that he would not be hurried.

"It is not possible for you to go inside it as everything is locked up," she replied. "But you can, of course, look at it from the outside."

She led the way with almost a bad grace to a door which lay on the other side of the Study and which took them straight out into the court-yard.

From this angle the barn seemed almost to dwarf the house.

As the Marquis looked at it he realised it was very old, the bricks between the ships' beams from which it was built were small and narrow, and were he knew, either Elizabethan or earlier.

He looked at it for some minutes, then glanced around the court-yard.

He saw on the other side of it there were a number of the white stones like those which decorated the flower-beds at the front, but which here were arranged in patterns of Naval symbols.

There was an anchor, life-size, gleaming white against the ground on which it had been fashioned, there was a Union Jack, the stripes making it not so effective as the anchor, and there was a more ambitious project in the shape of a sailing ship.

"I see you have very nautical tastes, Mrs. Wadebridge," the Marquis remarked.

"Those were done a long time ago by my brother and his friends when they were at home on leave."

As Mrs. Wadebridge spoke, she turned as if she would re-enter the house, but Anthony gave an exclamation.

"Look!" he said. "What is that?"

He pointed as he spoke, to a large lime tree which stood in a corner of the court-yard.

The Marquis followed the direction of his finger and saw to his surprise a flash of brilliant colour amongst the leaves.

For a moment he could not think what it was. Then he said:

"Surely it is a parrot?"

"A parakeet to be correct," Mrs. Wadebridge replied.

"There is more than one," Anthony said. "Are they tame."

As if she was amused by his astonishment Mrs. Wadebridge walked towards the tree, then made several low sounds which were the exact replica of a parakeet's call.

As she did so, she held out her arms and from the tree came fluttering down towards her a number of the small brilliant birds with their crimson and green plumage which seemed strangely out of place in the English sunshine.

Two settled on her hands, two more on each of her arms, and another on her shoulder.

With her green gown she made a strange but very lovely picture as she stood holding them with her head thrown back to look at several other parakeets which were circling overhead.

Both the Marquis and Anthony stared entranced until she shook herself free of them saying as she did so:

"It is too early for food. You will have to wait."

They flew away back into the tree from which they had come and the Marquis said:

"If I had not seen that with my own eyes, I would not have believed it!"

"Nor would I," Anthony agreed. "You must have had them for a long time for them to come when you call them."

"I think they know I love them," Mrs. Wadebridge said simply.

Now she walked determinedly back into the house and when they reached the hall she waited for the Marquis to make his farewells.

"I shall look forward to tomorrow evening," he said politely, "and I am extremely relieved, Mrs. Wadebridge, to know that so far, you have not been troubled by Highwaymen. At the same time, I would advise you to keep your doors locked."

"I will do that," Mrs. Wadebridge replied.

She walked to the door and waited politely as the Marquis and Sir Anthony mounted their horses.

As they drove them towards the drive, the Marquis looked again at the neat flower-beds.

'It must have taken a lot of work to keep them in such perfect condition,' he thought.

Then, lying beside the stones he saw a strange object.

For a moment he wondered what it was. Then he realised it was a wooden leg, the type that was worn by a man who had had his own limb amputated.

It was lying on the small grass path and it struck the Marquis that it had been thrown down hastily and forgotten.

He did not speak and when they were through the gates, Anthony exclaimed:

"Good Heavens, Justin! Who would have thought we would have found anything so lovely, so exquisite in the wilds of Sussex? I have never seen such eyes! I cannot imagine why you did not ask her to dinner this evening instead of our having to wait until tomorrow night."

"For God's sake, Anthony, you know she is married," the Marquis replied. "You have just tumbled out of one mess with Lucy Bicester. You cannot make a fool of yourself for a second time!"

He spoke so aggressively that Anthony looked at him in surprise.

"Really, Justin, I have never known you behave like a spoil-sport before! Here are you and I with nothing to do except worry about some Highwayman we are never likely to catch. We see the prettiest girl we have seen in a month of Sundays, and you say it is 'hands off' because she has a husband!"

The Marquis did not reply and Anthony said:

"I cannot think what is the matter with you. Husbands have never worried you before, unless they were pointing a pistol at your heart."

The Marquis still made no answer but merely spurred his

horse forward and Anthony had some difficulty in keeping up with him.

As they neared Heathcliffe the Marquis asked:

"Did you notice how neat and tidy the garden was?"

"Of course I did!" Anthony replied. "In fact, I thought only a sailor could have kept it so 'spick and span'."

"Exactly!" the Marquis agreed. "But the only sailor we saw was the one who held the horses, and that is another thing – why should he be waiting for us when we arrived? And the door opened the moment we knocked on it."

Anthony looked at him.

"What are you trying to say?"

"It seemed strange," the Marquis answered, "but I am quite certain that Mrs. Waderbridge knew we were arriving."

"How on earth could she have known that?" Anthony asked.

The Marquis suddenly remembered the man he had seen riding away from the house as they arrived.

He tried to remember more clearly what he had looked like, and he was sure that from his clothes he had not been a gentleman, in which case he must have been a groom or a servant, and who else would have good horse-flesh except himself?

"What are you thinking?" Anthony asked curiously.

"I am not certain I can put it into words," the Marquis answered, "but I am becoming more and more convinced there is something going on which I cannot explain, but it is definitely out of the ordinary."

"I should jolly well think it is!" Anthony remarked. "It is not ordinary to find amazingly beautiful women who can call parakeets out of an English lime tree, and have them sitting tamely on their hands and arms."

He gave a sigh.

"I have never seen anything so beautiful as that girl looked."

"Woman!" the Marquis corrected.

"I bet you she is not a day over eighteen," Anthony said, "and she cannot have been married long. Once a woman is married, she looks married."

He paused as if searching for the right words, then went on:

"She loses something, the innocence which had made her appear untouched."

The Marquis looked at him with undisguised astonishment.

"You never cease to surprise me, Anthony," he said, "but I am rather inclined to agree with you although, as it happens, I have known very few young girls."

"There are very few as pretty as – what was her name? Ivana Wadebridge," Anthony replied.

"Well, you will see her tomorrow evening," the Marquis said. "In the meantime I intend to look further afield for our Highwaymen, and I have no intention of letting a pretty face and a lot of parakeets divert me from tracking them down."

Anthony did not argue, but the Marquis had the feeling he thought it was a forlorn hope.

The next day the Marquis and Anthony drove miles in their efforts to find anyone who had seen the Highwaymen.

Despite Mr. Markham's discouraging information that they had few neighbours, the Marquis made enquiries in the neighbouring villages and personally visited a number of people living on small farms or on the outskirts of hamlets, who were both astonished and gratified to be called on by the owner of Veryan.

They had all heard of his father, they all admired Heathcliffe and they fawned on the Marquis in a manner which Anthony told him was extremely bad for him.

"It is all inflating to your ego," he said when they were going home after a fruitless day on which the Marquis had gained no information, but collected a great number of admirers.

"I thought they were very pleasant," the Marquis said. "The only trouble is that none of them have heard of the Highwaymen."

"I begin to think they do not exist," Anthony replied. "The wine was too good and we just dreamt the whole incident."

"In which case I would like back my watch and my snuff-boxes," the Marquis said sharply.

"Well, we can forget Highwaymen for tonight and concentrate on the blue-eyed beauty. As she had a magic way with parakeets, she might be clairvoyant enough to tell us where they are hiding."

The Marquis laughed.

"She might be hiding a dozen more in that huge barn of hers."

Even as he spoke he stiffened.

He was remembering something; something which he had not thought about until this moment.

"What is it?" Anthony asked.

"Do you know," the Marquis said, "when she had those parakeets fluttering all around her, I am convinced we were not the only people watching them."

"What do you mean by that?" Anthony asked.

"Now I think of it I am almost sure, although it made no impression on me at the time, that I saw a face at one of the windows in the barn."

"She said it was locked up."

"I know. She also said that she and her old Nurse were alone in the house. If that is true, where was the man to whom the wooden leg belonged?"

"He was obviously a gardener," Anthony said.

"May be, but one gardener could not have kept that garden as tidy as we saw it to be. What is more, I do not believe her old nurse, who must be over sixty, could have polished those stairs, the furniture, the floors and the brass. I could see my face in them."

"You are concocting a good story," Anthony laughed. "But at the same time, if you ask me, you are making mountains out of molehills. Ivana is a simple, charming, open country girl with blue eyes, and if you think she has Highwaymen locked up in her barn . . ."

"It is as likely as if she had parakeets in a lime tree!" the Marquis finished before Anthony could end the sentence himself.

"All right, you can cross-examine her tonight, and I bet you ten sovereigns she will not give you a single clue."

"Taken!" the Marquis said.

"If we are taking sides," Anthony warned. "I shall align myself with Ivana against you, and you will certainly get nowhere."

"That is a challenge!" the Marquis smiled, "and you know I can never resist one!"

. . . .

Dressing for dinner in the best gown she had which was a very simple one, Ivana listened to Nanny saying over and over again that she had been foolish to accept the Marquis's invitation.

"Why do you think he has asked you except to make trouble?" the old woman enquired.

"It would seem very unfriendly if I had refused," Ivana replied.

She sat down suddenly on the stool in front of the mirror and looking at her reflection said:

"Perhaps it was wrong . . but at the time I could think of no . . plausible reason for . . refusing."

"We could send a message to say you are feeling ill."

Ivana thought of the Marquis's firm mouth and had the feeling that if he wanted her to dine with him he would go on asking her until she had run out of excuses and there was nothing she could do but accept.

"I will go and get it over with," she said. "After all, it will be an ordinary social evening with doubtless both fine gentlemen yawning with boredom by the time we reach the dessert."

"I hopes that's what'll happen," Nanny snapped. "At the

same time, if you ask me, it's too much to hope for!"

Ivana laughed.

"It is no use being faint-hearted now, Nanny, when we have been through so much," she said, "and it is not like you to be afraid of anyone, even the Marquis."

As she spoke Ivana thought she personally was, in fact, rather frightened.

She had heard about him all her life, but although she had known that he was good-looking, dashing, raffish and also brave, she had not expected him in the flesh to be quite so over-powering or indeed to be so handsome.

As many women had thought before her, the Marquis and Sir Anthony together were almost breathtaking.

Never had she imagined two men could look so elegant, almost dandifiedly smart, and at the same time, be so un-mistakably masculine.

There was no doubt, she thought when they had gone, that Sir Anthony had admired her, but she had the un-comfortable feeling that the Marquis was feeling something very different.

Could he be suspicious? And if so, of what?

She gave a cry of vexation when she realised after they had left that George's wooden leg had been left in the garden and he had hobbled away on his stick without it. Then when he realised what he had done, he was afraid to go back and fetch it.

Perhaps the Marquis had not seen it, but Ivana was sure his penetrating eyes which made her feel shy and rather frightened had missed nothing, especially something he was not meant to see.

She thought now perhaps it had been a mistake to call the parakeets down from the tree, but at least it had diverted the gentlemen's attention.

She had been worried the rest of the day after they had gone and found it hard to sleep last night. Now Nanny had grumbled and complained all the time she was pressing her gown.

"Why can't we be left in peace?" she asked. "Who'd have imagined the Marquis of Veryan would have come here? Your poor grandfather must be turning in his grave?"

"That is true enough, Nanny," Ivana agreed. "For a Veryan to stand on the soil of Flagstaff House would be an insult in itself!"

But how could she carry on that ridiculous vendetta which, Ivana thought, had ruined her childhood because she was never allowed to go to Heathcliffe?

She remembered sitting on top of the wall and staring at it far away in the distance with longing eyes.

"Could I not just go to the stables to see the horses, Grandpapa?" she had asked once.

The request had called down an avalanche of abuse upon her head, which had left her in tears and made her determined she would never mention Heathcliffe again.

Of course tales of the Marquis had percolated into Flagstaff House, and anyway they talked of nothing else in the village.

When he was at Brighton with the Prince of Wales the local people who saw him reported his extravagance, the lovely ladies he squired and the way his horses romped home first at Lewes Races.

Now Ivana thought, she had not only seen him but was to dine with him.

She looked at herself in the mirror, anxiously wondering if because she had nothing smart or fashionable to wear, she would be wise to listen to Nanny and stay at home.

"Perhaps he will despise me for being so countrified," she told herself, "and that will be a good thing, for then he will leave me alone."

She had the feeling that even if the Marquis decided to do that his friend, Sir Anthony, would be more concerned with her face than what she was wearing.

Anyway, when the carriage arrived there was nothing she could do but pick up the scarf which matched her gown and let Nanny put a plain woollen shawl over her shoulders to keep her warm during the short drive to Heathcliffe.

"Now be careful what you says, dearie," Nanny admonished, "and come home as soon as you can. I'll be praying everything will be all right and there's no nasty pitfalls when you least expect them."

"Yes, do that, Nanny."

Ivana kissed her old Nurse's cheek and stepped into the carriage which was more comfortable and luxurious than any carriage she had ever travelled in before.

When she reached Heathcliffe to find four footmen on duty in the Hall and Travers greeting her politely, she had a sudden impulse to run away and return to the quiet security of Flagstaff House.

Then pride made her lift her chin and she followed Travers towards the Drawing-Room asking herself why should she be afraid of the Marquis or any other man.

"Mrs. Wadebridge, M'Lord!" Travers announced.

The Marquis walked towards her and Ivana thought it would be impossible for a man to look more magnificent and it was difficult not to be aware how drab and insignificant she must look beside him.

As it happened, the blue gown which Nanny had made for her the previous year, gave her a picture-like appearance so that she might have stepped down from one of the portraits on the walls of Veryan.

"She should be painted by Sir Joshua Reynolds," the Marquis thought to himself.

He was aware that while he bowed in response to her curtsey, Anthony taking advantage of the fact that she was a married woman, kissed her hand.

"Come and sit down," he was saying. "I feel sure you would enjoy a glass of champagne."

"It would certainly be a treat," Ivana replied.

"I suppose as your house is a sort of Naval establishment your guests are provided only with rum!" Anthony suggested, his eyes twinkling.

"In case you are suspecting we have not paid Excise Duty," Ivana flashed, "let me inform you, Sir Anthony, sailors are just as civilised in their tastes as soldiers!"

"That is right, Mrs. Wadebridge," the Marquis agreed. "Do not let him tease you. And to prove that soldiers can still appreciate the sea, I hope you will enjoy after dinner looking at the ship pictures which this house contains."

"They are superb!" Ivana said, and added quickly: "So I have always been told."

There was just a faint pause before the last words and the Marquis looked at her enquiringly.

He thought the colour rose in her face, but she turned her head to speak to Anthony and he was not certain.

He however, watched her every move and he was sure that she knew the way to the Dining-Room. He also thought, although he could not be certain that once during the evening a look passed between her and Travers that made him sure they had met before.

"I believe my agent Markham, Mrs. Wadebridge," he said apropos of nothing, "was a friend of your father's?"

For a moment he thought Ivana Wadebridge's eyes widened, then she asked:

"Did he tell you so?"

"He spoke of your father in glowing terms, so that I was sure they were acquainted, and Markham agreed that was so."

"I dare say they met," Ivana said vaguely, "especially as we shop in the same village."

The Marquis though this told him nothing, but determined to attack he asked:

"Are you going to tell me, Mrs. Wadebridge, that this is your first visit to Heathcliffe?"

Ivana laughed quite naturally.

"All my life," she said, "there was not an angel with a flaming sword keeping me away but a Naval gun pointing directly at my back if I should so much as walk in the direction of Heathcliffe!"

The way she had answered his question made it impossible for the Marquis to press her further, and when dinner was finished and port was on the table, she rose to her feet to say:

"I think, My Lord, I should withdraw in the correct fashion and wait for you in the Drawing-Room."

"I think we will start by sitting in the Library," the Marquis replied. "I want to show you from where the snuff-boxes were taken and you can see how devastatingly empty the place is."

"Then I will wait for you in the Library," Ivana smiled.

She went from the Dining-Room and only when she had been gone for some minutes did the Marquis realise that she had not asked where the Library was.

At the same time, he told himself there would be a footman on duty in the hall and she could ask him.

Because it was insistent in his mind, he said to Anthony: "I am certain there is something strange about this young woman. I am sure she is not what she appears."

"I am perfectly happy with her as she is," Anthony said. "I find her charming, amusing and very, very lovely. Good God, Justin, what else do you expect?"

"That is the trouble, I do not know what I expect," the Marquis replied. "I just feel in the back of my mind, or in my bones, as my father used to say, that everything is not as it should be and I am being deceived."

"It is Rose who has made you feel like that," Anthony said. "You think because she tricked you that everybody else has the same idea. You look for footprints, criminals behind every door, and doubtless smugglers in the cellar. I will make love to Ivana and tell her I think she is adorable!"

For some reason Anthony's answer annoyed the Marquis.

He put down his glass and rose from the table and without speaking walked from the Dining-Room, while Anthony waited to pour himself another glass of port from the decanter before he followed him.

The Marquis found Ivana in the Library.

She was sitting in the window and not, as he thought critically, as any other intelligent woman would have been looking at the books and the pictures.

He walked across the room to join her but she did not turn her head. Instead looking at the trees silhouetted against the dusk.

"It is so beautiful here. How can you possibly stay away for five years from a place that is so lovely and peaceful?"

"I have been thinking since I came back that I have been very remiss in not returning before."

"I think most people would be grateful that the place they remembered had changed so little."

"But there are changes!" the Marquis objected.

"What sort of changes?"

"A lot of the old servants have gone, for one thing. I thought to see familiar faces, but instead Bateman the Butler has retired."

"You will find him in the village."

"You know him?"

"Yes, of course."

"Why of course?"

"Because living here I know everyone in the village."

"Then perhaps you can tell me what has happened to the footmen we used to have."

Ivana stiffened for a moment, then she said in a very different tone:

"I am sure your agent, My Lord, will give you any information you require about the servants in the house, but now I think I should go home."

Her last words were heard by Anthony as he came into the Library.

"Go home?" he echoed. "That is ridiculous! We have a lot to show you, have we not Justin? The pictures for instance, and a lot of other things I think you will find fascinating."

"I am sorry," Ivana said, "but you must excuse me because I have a headache. I think perhaps it is the heat. It has been excessively hot today."

77

"If you must go," Anthony said, "I will take you back. I would not like to think of you driving alone now it is dark."

"I shall be perfectly all right," Ivana answered hastily.

"You cannot be sure of that. After all, the Highwaymen may be lurking in the bushes, waiting to make you 'stand and deliver' while they take your jewels and your money."

Ivana laughed.

"Then they will certainly be disappointed, for I have neither."

"You are too pretty to be alone," Anthony reiterated. "If Justin and I had not been so thoughtless one of us would have come to fetch you."

"I shall be perfectly safe in such a magnificent carriage with Goddard driving."

It registered with the Marquis that she knew the coachman's name.

Again the explanation perhaps lay in tht fact that they had met in the village, but Goddard and his family lived in a house on the other side of the stables and there was therefore no reason for Mrs. Wadebridge to see them unless she came to Heathcliffe.

"I tell you what we will do," the Marquis said. "We will drive Mrs. Wadebridge back in the Phaeton, unless she feels it would be too cold?"

"It will certainly not be that," Ivana replied, "and I would really love to drive in your Phaeton."

The Marquis rang the bell and while he gave the order for the Phaeton to be brought to the front door, Anthony drew Ivana across the room to look at one of the pictures.

As she made normal conversation about the painting he stood looking down at her with what the Marquis told himself was a sloppy expression on his face.

"You have not finished your port, Anthony," he remarked, as if he wished to intrude on what appeared to be a romantic interlude.

With an obvious effort, but because he knew the Marquis

78

had given him a command, Anthony crossed the room and took up the glass he had left on the side-table.

The Marquis stood beside Ivana.

"I have not told you of the long and arduous search we have made today for the Highwaymen."

"Search for the Highwaymen?"

"Anthony and I drove all over the County calling on different people, making enquiries at village Inns. It was really extraordinary that nobody had ever heard of the gang."

"Perhaps they are newcomers."

"It seems strange they should choose Heathcliffe for their first operation when Brighton is teeming with jewels of every description, fat purses filled with golden guineas, and of course, an enormous amount of treasures in the Royal Pavilion."

"For all we know," Ivana replied, "the Highwaymen may be there at this very moment, holding up the Prince of Wales himself!"

"There is always that possibility," the Marquis agreed, "but it still seems to me strange that in the whole of Sussex they should come to Heathcliffe the very night I return after a lapse of five years."

"Surely, My Lord, they were as surprised to see you as you were to see them?" Ivana suggested.

There was a smile on her lips that told the Marquis she was very pleased about something and he wondered what it could be.

Then she moved towards the empty cabinet to lay her hand for a moment on the glass top.

"Are you very disconsolate at losing the snuff-boxes that you have neglected for so many years?" she enquired.

The Marquis was aware there was a sting in the question and he replied sharply:

"Apart from their value they meant a great deal to me because my father was so fond of them."

"In which case surely you would have wished to remove

79

them to one of your other houses where you could see them more frequently."

The Marquis had the feeling that she was being definitely hostile, and now he looked into her eyes as he said:

"I think, Mrs. Wadebridge, you are taking me to task not only for neglecting the snuff-boxes, but also for neglecting Heathcliffe. Could that be right?"

"How could I presume to question anything Your Lordship does?" Ivana replied. "But of course, if I have made you feel guilty I can only apologise."

The Marquis's lips twisted and he was trying to think of a scathing reply, as Travers announced:

"The Phaeton is at the door, My Lord!"

"Then I must go," Mrs. Wadebridge said. "I am sorry if I seem rude, but actually I do not like leaving my old Nanny alone for long. She becomes nervous."

"Of what?" the Marquis enquired.

He saw Mrs. Wadebridge's dimples as she answered:

"The dark. Nanny believes in ghosts and spirits who walk by night. What else can you imagine would perturb her?"

There was a glint in her blue eyes which left the Marquis feeling as if they crossed swords.

It gave him a strange feeling of elation.

He did not know why, but instead of dampening down his instinct to probe deeper she had positively accentuated it.

They walked into the Hall and Travers put her shawl around Ivana's shoulders.

"Thank you, Travers," she said quietly.

As they walked to the Phaeton the Marquis was trying to remember if he had mentioned Travers by name during dinner.

He was almost certain he had not, and yet again there was no reason why she should not know his Butler's name. He too must shop in the village.

Ivana sat between the two men on the way back and the Marquis was aware that Anthony was whispering compliments in her ear and she was laughing at him.

It struck him that she was certainly not the shy, frightened country-girl he had expected her to be. She seemed sure of herself although there was a very young, untouched look about her which the Marquis had not seen for many years.

The sophisticated women like Lady Rose with whom he made love, certainly did not have it, and it suddenly struck him that considering how few, if any, cosmetics Ivana used, her face would certainly not look smudged in the morning, and he was quite certain that she did not snore.

It did not take them long to reach Flagstaff House and the Marquis negotiated the narrow drive most skilfully.

Ivana stepped out to thank them most profusely for a delightful evening.

"I must see you again very soon," Anthony said in a low voice as he took her to the door.

Ivana was saved from answering because Nanny was standing there looking, he thought, like a ruffled hen who had been worrying over her one chick.

"Good-night, Sir Anthony," Ivana said.

He kissed her hand and she looked to where the Marquis was still sitting in the Phaeton, controlling the horses.

"Good-night, My Lord."

He swept his hat from his head.

"Good-night, Mrs. Wadebridge."

Ivana went into the house and Anthony climbed back into the Phaeton.

With some skill the Marquis managed to turn the horses so that the wheels of the Phaeton did not go over the closely cut grass or the white painted stones.

They drove through the gates, then as they turned towards Heathcliffe he looked back at the house.

From the angle they had reached he could just see the end of the great barn protruding behind it. Then as he looked he was aware with a sudden start of satisfaction that in one of its windows there was a light.

CHAPTER FOUR

The Marquis awoke in the morning with a feeling of excitement which he had not known for years.

He had been a long time in going to sleep, finding it difficult to see anything but Ivana's face and her expressive eyes.

He kept remembering how frightened she had seemed when he and Anthony had first walked into her Drawing-Room at the Manor and, the more he thought over the way they had been received, the more he was absolutely convinced that she and her Nurse had been expecting them.

It was not really surprising that the Nurse had called him 'M'Lord' and known who he was.

After all, she had lived at Flagstaff House for years and she would have been well aware there was nobody else in the neighbourhood with his appearance or consequence.

Far more significant was the fact that a groom had been waiting, the front door had been opened immediately and Ivana was sitting like an elegant lady in her Drawing-Room.

He was quite sure she would be far too active and busy even in her restricted life to sit doing nothing at any time of the day, yet the difficulty was how to prove it.

When she stood calling the parakeets so that they fluttered down to her from the tree she had made, the Marquis thought, an inerasable picture.

Then suddenly he remembered a conversation she had with Anthony to which he had hardly listened at the time but which now came into his mind so that he found himself grasping at it almost as if it was a raft in a rough sea.

They had been talking together as they walked back to

the house after she had released the parakeets and Anthony had asked:

"You must have practised for years, Mrs. Wadebridge, to imitate the sound they make so accurately."

If the Marquis remembered correctly she had replied with a light laugh:

"Oh, I am a good mimic."

He had been so preoccupied at the time, thinking of the barn and the strange Naval patterns in the court-yard, that it had been of no particular consequence for him.

Now he thought that the call of the parakeet was a deep note and wondered whether it would be possible for a woman who was a mimic to imitate a man's deep voice?

Then he told himself this was too far-fetched even for his credibility. It must be impossible for anyone so feminine and indeed so beautiful as Ivana Wadebridge to disguise herself as a Highwayman.

But the thought persisted, although he decided in the morning light, as his idea seemed even more exaggerated than it had in the dark, that he would not mention what he had been thinking to Anthony.

At breakfast as Anthony helped himself liberally to a dish of kidneys and fresh mushrooms, he said:

"What excitements have you planned for today? More sleuthing? I am beginning to acquire an aptitude for it."

The Marquis merely smiled and Anthony continued:

"As far as I am concerned I would like to visit Flagstaff House again and talk to the dark, blue-eyed beauty I find so infinitely beguiling."

The Marquis was about to agree that he too wished to see Mrs. Wadebridge again when he realised that Travers was in the room.

"I have a different plan . . ." he began, only to be interrupted by Anthony who said:

"Do not take up that prosaic attitude again, Justin."

He looked up as he spoke and saw that the Marquis was frowning at him.

"What is upsetting you?" he asked, only to realise he was being indiscreet and relapsed into silence.

They talked of horses and what had been in the newspapers of the day before.

They only arrived at Heathcliffe late in the afternooon because a groom had to fetch them from Brighton.

When the two men moved from the Dining-Room into the Library Anthony asked:

"What is going on? Why were you frowning at me and making secret signs during breakfast?"

The Marquis glanced to see if the door was shut behind him, then he said:

"Travers was in the room."

'I gathered after you had indicated I was putting my foot in it, that was the reason you were being so mysterious," Anthony said, "but why? What has Travers to do with it?"

"I have no reason to think it was he who sent a message to Flagstaff House yesterday when we were on our way to call there. In fact, I am almost certain it was Markham. But if we do pay the blue-eyed beauty a visit, I wish to do so without her being forewarned."

"Good Heavens, Justin, this is really cloak and dagger stuff!" Anthony jeered. "If you ask me, you are barking up the wrong tree. I am quite certain that Blue Eyes is as pure as driven snow, and as guileless as a child."

"She has a husband," the Marquis said dryly, "a servant who leaves a wooden leg in the garden, and someone who sleeps in the locked barn."

"How do you know that?" Anthony asked almost truculently.

"There was a light in the window when we left there last night."

"You did not tell me."

"I was thinking about it, wondering why Mrs. Wadebridge should have lied, wondering what exactly she is hiding."

There was silence for a moment. Then Anthony said:

"You are beginning to intrigue me, Justin, and by the way I think you owe me ten guineas."

"Why?"

"Because as far as I am concerned she gave you no clues last night and that was our bet."

The Marquis sighed.

"I suppose I shall have to admit that you are right. At the same time I think she was particularly adroit at avoiding committing herself on several questions I asked her."

"If later you can prove that I was not entitled to it, I can pay you back," Anthony said, "but in the meantime, hand over what you owe me."

The Marquis smiled as he sat down at his writing-table.

"You will take an I.O.U.?"

"I suppose I must trust you," Anthony joked.

The Marquis took the piece of paper on which he had written the sum he owed his friend and folding it with a practised hand into a paper dart, threw it across the room at him.

"Would you like to bet on an outside chance?" he asked.

"What is it?" Anthony questioned.

"That either Mrs. Wadebridge, or perhaps her husband, is the Highwayman we are seeking!"

Anthony's mouth gaped open in sheer astonishment. Then he replied:

"Now you are really pulling my leg!"

"No, I am serious," the Marquis contradicted. "Do you remember yesterday she told you she was a mimic? And who is she hiding in the barn – her husband?"

"Why on earth should she be doing that?"

"I have no idea, unless he is a deserter from the Navy."

"That does not sound much like a Wadebridge to me with all their sea-faring traditions."

"It would be all the more reason if he was in trouble."

"Yes, of course. I see your point, but it seems very far-fetched. So are the parakeets, a light in the barn which we were told was locked, a Highwayman walking into the

Dining-Room when we are at dinner, and Ivana Wadebridge herself, if it comes to that."

Anthony threw up his hands.

"I agree. The whole thing is unreal, preposterous and could only happen in our dreams."

Without speaking the Marquis glanced towards the empty cabinet which had held his father's snuff-boxes.

"All right," Anthony capitulated. "You win! But because I refuse to believe anything you tell me, I bet you £50 that Ivana Wadebridge is not a Highwayman, although I am not sure I can say the same about her husband."

"Agreed," the Marquis said, "and we will take another step forward in our investigations."

"Where to?"

"I want to visit Bateman who was the Butler at Heath-cliffe for at least twenty-five years and who was here on my last visit."

"Very well," Anthony said. "Have you ordered the horses?"

"They should be at the door," the Marquis replied.

. . . .

They rode through the Park, taking the longest way to the village so that they could gallop and take the first crispness out of their mounts.

As they rode between the trees they disturbed the spotted deer lying in the shade. The Marquis realised the herds had increased enormously since his father's day and thought he must speak to the game-keepers about them.

There were really a lot of people he should have seen since he arrived had he not been so busy trying to track down the Highwayman.

When he thought about it, he realised he should have congratulated the Head Gardener on the gardens, talked to his game-keepers and foresters, and had a report on the con-ditions of the farms.

He was surprised that Markham had not suggested it to him, but he supposed the agent was afraid that he might find it boring and was anxious for him to enjoy himself at Heathcliffe after an absence of so many years rather than immediately having to face domestic problems.

'Nevertheless,' the Marquis thought, 'it is something I must do, and as Anthony and I will not be leaving quickly there is plenty of time.'

They trotted through the gates outside which began the small, rather straggly village.

Most of the houses with their attractive thatched roofs had been built by the late Marquis for pensioners.

They all had small gardens filled with flowers and were clustered round the grey stone Norman Church which had stood there long before Heathcliffe was built.

It struck the Marquis that the tombstones which he had noticed when he used to accompany his grandfather to Church on Sundays must have been erected by the Wade-bridges.

It interested him to think that family had been there long before the Veryans, almost like usurpers, had taken over their land and the prestige of being the most important people in the vicinity.

It did not surprise him that the old Admiral hated his father, and he wondered what Ivana felt about him personally.

He was almost certain, although he could not be sure, that her feelings were those of fear rather than of dislike.

He saw a man walking in the village and realised from his appearance he was a clergyman.

The Marquis drew up his horse beside him.

"Are you the Vicar of this Parish?" he enquired.

The Cleric looked up with some surprise. Then the expression of enquiry on his face changed to one of recognition.

"I am," he said, "and I think you must be the Marquis of Veryan."

"That is correct," the Marquis answered, "although I am surprised you should recognise me."

The Vicar smiled.

"It is not a question of recognition, My Lord," he said. "I heard you had arrived at Heathcliffe, and you have a distinct look of your father about you."

"You knew my father?"

"Only in the last two years of His Lordship's life," the Vicar replied, "and may I say it is very pleasant to think there is a Veryan at Heathcliffe again."

"Thank you, Vicar," the Marquis answered, "I realise I have been away too long. As it happens at this moment I wish to call on Bateman who I learn has retired from my service. Can you tell me in which cottage he lives?"

"Haytop Cottage," the Vicar answered, pointing to the one in question, "but you will find he is not very well, poor fellow."

"I am sorry to hear that," the Marquis replied. "Was ill health the reason for his retirement?"

The Vicar hesitated. Then as the Marquis waited he said after a moment:

"Has not Mr. Markham informed Your Lordship of the exact circumstances?"

"No," the Marquis replied, "and I would be grateful if you would do so."

He dismounted as he spoke to stand by the side of the Vicar who was a middle-aged man, his hair just beginning to turn grey.

"I think Mr. Markham should have told you, My Lord," the Vicar began after a moment's hesitation, "that Bateman was drinking too much and was therefore incapable of carrying out his duties."

"Drinking!" the Marquis exclaimed.

"I hope Your Lordship will not think I am criticising in any way," the Vicar said, "but quite frankly he did not have enough to do, and since he was also, I understand, in charge of the cellar, the temptation was too great for him."

"A pity," the Marquis remarked. "I always thought him a good man."

"He was," the Vicar agreed, "but Satan, My Lord, finds mischief for idle hands."

The Marquis's lips tightened and he said:

"Haytop Cottage, you say. Well, thank you, Vicar, I am glad to have met you."

"And I you, My Lord," the Vicar replied.

The Marquis, holding his horse's rein, moved along the road to the gate of the cottage the Vicar had indicated.

When he reached it he looked around and saw on the other side of the road there were several small boys staring with admiration at the horses.

He beckoned the tallest of them who crossed the road eagerly.

"I want you to hold my horse," the Marquis said. "Do you understand horses and how to be quiet and gentle with them?"

"Aye, Sir."

"Just take him by the bridle and if he becomes restless you can walk him a little way up the road, as far as the Church and back again. Do you understand?"

"Aye, Sir."

Seeing what the Marquis was doing Anthony did the same, and the two boys, pink with excitement were patting the horses and making a fuss of them as the Marquis and Anthony walked up the small flagged path of the black and white painted cottage.

The door was opened by a buxom young woman of about thirty who was overwhelmed by their appearance and curtsied awkwardly, being for the moment obviously too tongue-tied to be able to say anything.

"I am the Marquis of Veryan, and I would like to see Bateman. Are you his daughter?"

"N . no, M'Lord . . his niece. Oi give up me position up at the 'ouse to look after him."

'You were at Heathcliffe?'

'Aye, M'Lord."

"I have missed your uncle since I returned. May I talk to him?

The woman hestiated for a moment.

"Your Lordship might foind 'im somewhat changed."

"I understand," the Marquis said. "Where will he be?"

In answer the woman crossed the small kitchen and opened the door at the back of it. It led into a small but clean bedroom in which the old Butler, wearing a red flannel nightshirt, was lying.

It was hard to recognise the man who he had always thought had the somewhat pontifical look of an Archbishop.

His face was now red and puffed, his nose swollen, and both his hands and his head seemed to shake as the Marquis moved into the room.

" 'Ere's His Lordship t'see ye, Uncle," the woman said.

She returned to the kitchen, leaving the Marquis and Anthony alone with Bateman.

There were two chairs and as the Marquis brought his nearer to the bed, he saw the old Butler's eyes were bloodshot and was quite certain that although he was bedridden, he had not given up his drinking habits.

"I am sorry to see you in such a state, Bateman," he said. "I missed you when I returned to Heathcliffe. The house does not seem the same without you."

"It's kind of Your Lordship to say so, M'Lord," Bateman replied. "I used to plan how I'd have everythin' ready for Your Lordship when you paid us a visit, but I were taken ill an' Mr. Markham gave me this cottage."

He paused for a moment, Then said in a resentful tone:

"Not that it didn't suit him to be rid of me!"

He slurred his words slightly and the Marquis was aware that early though it was in the morning, he must have already been drinking unless it was a hang-over from the night before.

It seemed extraordinary that his niece should allow him to drink to excess when he was in fact an invalid, but the Marquis was more interested at the moment in what he had just said.

"Why should it suit Mr. Markham to retire you?" He asked.

"That's somethin' Your Lordship'll have to find out for yourself," Bateman replied.

"I have known you long enough, Bateman," the Marquis said, "to know that my father trusted you as I do, and I always believed you were devoted to Heathcliffe."

"I thought of it as me home, M'Lord," Bateman replied, "and His late Lordship were a grand gentleman, no-one can deny that."

"I agree with you," the Marquis said quietly. "But what I am trying to find out is if anything went wrong after he died, and why you are no longer serving me as I would like you to do."

"It weren't fair, M'Lord. After Cobbler and Wilkins and the other two footmen went to the war, they weren't replaced. For a while I managed on me own, but it wasn't easy to keep things as Your Lordship'd have wanted."

"Cobbler and Wilkins were not replaced?" the Marquis asked.

'No, M'Lord. They went first, then James, then Nicholson – not that he was ever much good. Had a head like a sieve, he had. I'd tried to carry on, M'Lord, but 'twere too much for me."

"You told Mr. Markham so?"

"Told him? Over and over again I tells him, but he didn't want to listen."

There was a pause before Bateman went on:

"He had reasons for not listening – I knows that but 'twere not fair on me, M'Lord."

"What reasons did he have?" the Marquis questioned.

He spoke sharply, then realised it had been a mistake.

Bateman stiffened and his confidential air vanished. There was a look in his eyes as if he remembered something and became wary.

He pushed himself back against the pillows.

"My niece'd say I were talking too much, M'Lord," he said in a different tone. "I gets muddled in me 'ead at times. I've nothing to say against Mr. Markham. Very generous he is to me – very!"

This was a complete change of front and the Marquis thought it best not to comment on it.

He decided he could get no more out of Bateman and it would be a mistake to press him.

Instead he rose to his feet.

"I am glad to have seen you, Bateman," he said. "You must hurry and get well. I would like to see you back at Heathcliffe."

" 'Tis too late, M'Lord. Too late now!"

The Marquis followed by Anthony went from the room into the kitchen where Bateman's niece was busy at the stove.

"I am sorry to see your uncle in such a state," the Marquis said.

She did not reply and he added:

"Surely it is a mistake for him to have so much to drink?"

The woman made a restless movement and averted her eyes.

"There's nothing I can do about it, M'Lord."

"Except prevent him from having it," the Marquis remarked. "How does he get hold of it and how can you afford what it costs?"

There was an expression on her face which he knew was one of obstinancy, and at the same time, of fear.

She remained silent and after a moment the Marquis said:

"I gather you do not intend to confide in me?"

"No, M'Lord. It's impossible!"

The Marquis drew two guineas from his vest pocket and put them on the table.

"Spend it on luxuries for your uncle," he said, "but not on drink of any sort. Is that understood?"

'Aye, M'Lord, and thank ye."

She curtsied again as the Marquis and Anthony left.

They rewarded the small boys who had held their horses and rode away in silence.

Only when they were clear of the village did Anthony say:

"What do you think all that meant?"

"I am not certain," the Marquis replied, "but it has certainly given me a lot to think about."

They rode back into the Park and Anthony instinctively turned his horse in the direction of Flagstaff House, but the Marquis said:

"I do not wish to see Mrs. Wadebridge today. I want to sort out my ideas and try to find out more about Bateman."

"All right," Anthony conceded with an ill grace. "Where next?"

"I think Grimshaw, my Head Gardener," the Marquis replied. "At least he has not been deposed or retired."

"I cannot imagine he is short-handed," Anthony said, "I have never seen a garden kept better except perhaps that of Flagstaff House."

"I hope Grimshaw can enlighten us on that," the Marquis suggested.

They rode back towards the house, and the Marquis led the way through the fields behind the stables to where a quarter of a mile from Heathcliffe hidden behind the high walls of the Kitchen-Garden, was a red brick house which had always belonged to the Head Gardener.

Once again they dismounted and now they saw a man wheeling a barrow loaded with rubbish out towards a dump outside the walls and called him to attend to their horses.

One look at him told the Marquis he was a Naval type and it was also obvious that he walked with a limp.

He did not intend however to question any of the under-gardeners until he had talked to Grimshaw, and walking

93

into the large walled-in-garden, the Marquis saw him at the far end of it.

He certainly had no complaints about the garden itself. It was a model of neatness with every possible inch cultivated.

Even the panes of the green-houses seemed to gleam in the sunshine as if they were exceptionally clean, and the fruit trees looked as if they were regimented into producing larger and more colourful fruit than any trees the Marquis had ever seen before.

Grimshaw looked much older than the Marquis remembered, but he was obviously pleased to see him.

"It be a soight for sore eyes, M'Lord, seein' ye after all these years!" he said, speaking his soft Sussex accent.

"I am glad to be back," the Marquis replied simply, "and I must congratulate you, Grimshaw on the garden. I have never seen it look more beautiful or in better trim."

"Oi'm glad Your Lordship be pleased."

"I cannot think how you have managed it when I understand for the last year or two of the war it was very difficult to get men."

"That moight be true for some, M'Lord, but not for us."

"Why not?" the Marquis enquired.

"Mr. Markham has managed to provide Oi wi' workers, one way or another."

"How did he manage to do that?" the Marquis asked.

"At first, M'Lord, they were always incapacitated. 'Th' halt, th' lame an' th' blind!' Oi used ter say laughing-like. Even so, Oi get some good work out of 'em."

"Are you telling me," the Marquis said, "that the men you have been employing are men who have been wounded in the war?"

"Yus, M'Lord. Sailors, but they be willin' t' work rather than starve, an' work Oi managed t' make 'em do!"

The Marquis did not reply and Grimshaw went on:

"O' course, since th' peace, M'Lord, we've 'ad whole men, so t' speak. Nothin' wrong wi' them, excep' many as never seen a spade nor a 'oe in 'is life. Oi teach them first, and 'though they sometimes grumbles at becoming land-lubbers, as they calls it, they be too glad t' be employed to be partic'lar."

"I must congratulate you once again on what you have achieved," the Marquis said. "Thank you, Grimshaw."

He was turning away when a thought struck him.

"By the way," he said, "how many men have you working under you at this particular moment?"

"Sixteen, M'Lord."

The Marquis walked back along the neat path between the vegetable beds with Anthony beside him.

"Cast-offs from the Navy!" he remarked in a low voice. "First those who had been wounded, then since April the men who are being made redundant."

"I have heard there are plenty of those," Anthony said. "In fact someone at the Club was saying only last week that we are disarming at an almost indecent speed."

The Marquis nodded.

"I heard Lord St. Vincent speak in the House of Lords," he said ruminatively. "He was absolutely insistent on drastic economies in Naval administration."

"I heard a worse story, now I think about it," Anthony said, "I was told that while all our ships are crying out for repairs, the dock-yard hands have been dismissed, contracts with private yards withdrawn and surplus stores sold off – in some cases to French agents!"

At this the Marquis stopped still to stare at his friend.

"And it was you who told me the other day we need not be afraid of Bonaparte!" he said accusingly. "I am sure he is replenishing his empty dock-yards and building ships at all possible speed."

"Now you are trying to make my flesh creep," Anthony retorted. "Go back to your sleuthing and remember you, at any rate, have benefited by having almost a ship's company working on your garden."

The Marquis did not reply. He was obviously deep in thought as they walked back towards the house.

By now it was luncheontime and before they went into the Dining-Room the Marquis said:

"Not a word in front of Travers of what we have discovered this morning."

"To hear is to obey!" Anthony replied lightly, "and when can we call on our new-found Beauty?"

"When I am ready to do so," the Marquis replied almost irritably.

"And when will that be?"

"When I have enough evidence to put her in the dock!" the Marquis answered.

"If I thought you meant what you said, I would feel inclined to knock you down!"

"You are welcome to try," the Marquis answered, "but remember we are very equal when it comes to pugilistic efforts, although I am quite prepared to offer you a little sword-play or, if you prefer, pistols at ten paces!"

"There you would undoubtedly claim an unfair advantage," Anthony said, "so I shall merely try to outwit you in some other way."

"Stop fighting against me. I want you with me," the Marquis said. "You must realise, Anthony, by now that something fantastic is happening. If we do not get to the bottom of it I swear it will leave me curious to to the end of my life."

"I am curious too," Anthony admitted. "I wonder what her husband is like?"

The Marquis picked up a cushion from the chair and flung it at his friend's head. Anthony caught it deftly and threw it back, but at that moment Travers announced that lucheon was served.

After an extremely good meal they went back to the Library and Anthony walking to the window asked:

"What now?"

As he spoke the Marquis made a sound that was almost a cry.

"What is the matter?" Anthony enquired.

"I am crazy!" the Marquis exclaimed, "and I certainly should have thought of it before."

"Thought of what?"

"Looking at Markham's accounts!"

"What will they tell you?"

"A great deal," the Marquis said. "Every month I have the accounts from all my estates sent to London. Sometimes I go through them personally, but otherwise I leave it to my secretary to see there is no unusual expenditure."

Anthony was listening intently as the Marquis went on:

"I distinctly remember looking at the accounts of Heath-cliffe two, or was it three months ago, and thinking that despite the rise in prices during the war, the expenses had remained more or less the same as when my father was in residence."

"What does that prove now?" Anthony asked.

"You must realise that these new men, and I swear there are more of them than were ever here before, have had to be paid."

There was silence for a moment. Then Anthony said:

"I see your reasoning – unless the 'halt and the lame' as your gardener referred to them, were paid less money than those who were in good shape."

"Even so, they should have been listed," the Marquis insisted. "So should the change of footmen."

"Well, let us get the ledgers and see for ourselves."

"That is just what I am thinking," the Marquis agreed. "At the same time, I think it would be a mistake to ask Markham to bring them to us."

"Why?"

"He might easily alter them, or say they were mislaid, or even that the Highwaymen had stolen them!"

"I see your point," Anthony answered. "Then how do you intend to go about getting hold of them?"

The Marquis thought for a moment, then said:

"We are now going, you and I, to make a tour of the house. We will saunter into the Hall and I shall say to you:

'By the way, Anthony, I have not been in the Orangery since I returned. I am sure Grimshaw has some magnificent plants there if the rest of the garden is anything to go by'."

"Go on," Anthony prompted. "What then?"

"The Orangery is in the direction of the Estate Office. We pass the Ballroom which has been shut up ever since I can remember, reach the Gun-Room where of course, we will look at the guns and pistols, then automatically walk into the Estate Office because it is next door. If Markham is there it will seem quite natural we should call in, in passing. If he is not we will find what we want."

"Excellent!" Anthony approved. "You are wasted in your present position. You should be head of the Bow Street Runners or take on the organisation of a National Police Force."

"That is something that may happen one day. They have talked about it long enough," the Marquis replied.

"One thing is quite certain," Anthony replied. "No-one in Parliament will vote any money for a new service at this moment."

"That is true," the Marquis agreed, "with the National Debt standing at double its pre-war figure."

Like two small boys playing a game, they set off to act the parts the Marquis had suggested.

There were two footmen in the Hall to hear them say they were going to the Orangery but the Marquis had the idea that Travers might be hovering somewhere within ear-shot.

The Orangery was, in fact, just as he had expected. The flowers and plants his father had collected were all in good order but although the Marquis could not be sure, he thought there were no new additions.

The Gun-Room in its turn was clean and tidy, but the sporting guns were out of date and the pistols almost ready for a Museum.

They did not stay long here, then as they moved into the passage, the Marquis said in a loud voice:

"While we are here I want you to look at an old map of

the estate which hangs in the Estate Office. It might show us where the Admiral's border lies."

"I would like to see that," Anthony replied.

The Marquis opened the door.

To his relief the office was empty, although there was a large ledger open on the desk with a quill pen beside it.

It looked in fact, as if Mr. Markham had been called away unexpectedly.

The Marquis went to the ledger and turning over the pages found it was what he wanted.

All the expenditure for the last four years was neatly listed and it was exactly as he had seen it when it had been sent to him in London.

He put the ledger under his arm and he and Anthony hurried back down the long passages which led into the Library.

There the Marquis sat down at his desk.

"Now we shall see for ourselves," he said, "exactly what has been happening."

He opened the ledger and turned back two years.

"Here is the household," he said. "And among the other names are Bateman, Cobbler, Wilkins, James and Nicholson."

"When is that?" Anthony enquired.

"The beginning of 1800."

The Marquis made as if to turn back a page, then said:

"I do not know when Cobbler, Wilkins and the other two left, but Bateman said he was short-handed before he retired, so we can start by seeing who replaced him."

He turned over the next few pages one by one until he came to the tail end of Markham's neat writing.

Then an expression on his face made Anthony ask quickly:

"What have you discovered?"

"According to the ledger," the Marquis said. "Cobbler, Wilkins, James and Nicholson are still in my employment.

They have been paid regularly and their wages are listed month by month!"

"Then Markham has been cheating you!" Anthony said.

"Exactly!" the Marquis replied, "and this is where I start my enquiries. Pull the bell!"

The note of command in his voice made Anthony realise how angry he was.

He knew if there was one thing that really infuriated him it was to think that he was being crooked or deceived in any way by those he trusted.

Neither man spoke until Travers opened the door.

"Tell Mr. Markham I wish to speak to him immediately!" the Marquis ordered.

"Very good, M'Lord."

Again there was silence and Anthony moved towards the window and feeling the atmosphere was oppressive, he opened one of the long windows which, like those in the Drawing-Room led directly onto the terrace above the lawns.

Then he turned back towards the Marquis.

"Do you wish me to stay?"

"Of course!" the Marquis replied.

The door opened and Mr. Markham came in.

It was obvious that he was apprehensive and the Marquis saw the fear on his face when he walked across the room to stand in front of the desk.

"I have been looking at your ledger, Markham," the Marquis began, "and I want an explanation as to why four footmen who are no longer in my employment are still listed here."

"It may have been remiss of me, My Lord," Mr. Markham replied in a voice that shook, "but as the other footmen I engaged in their place were taken on a temporary basis and received the same wages, it seemed unnecessary to change the names each time."

That was almost plausible, the Marquis thought, but he did not approve of such slip-shod methods.

"How is it that the men were only temporary, and why?"

'It is not easy to find men in this vicinity, My Lord, but I had to take what I could get and most of them were unsatisfactory."

The Marquis looked at his agent. While Markham was very pale, he was also sweating, and the Marquis was experienced enough in the handling of men to know that while he had a tight control on himself, he was, in fact, very frightened.

"I also see," the Marquis continued, "that you have not put on record when Bateman retired and Travers took his place."

"No, My Lord, for the same reason."

"But surely Travers seems a very experienced man, and you hoped he would stay?"

"I was not certain that he would do so, My Lord."

The Marquis turned over the pages.

"Now we come to the gardeners. Grimshaw tells me he has sixteen men working for him at the moment. Surely that is an abnormal amount?"

"Grimshaw has not complained that he is over-staffed."

"That is not the point," the Marquis snapped. "The wages you have drawn for the gardeners every week, have been for ten. How do you account for the extra?"

"Some are new-comers, My Lord, and I did not expect to pay them as much as those who have been with us for many years."

The Marquis looked at the names and turned back the ledger to its beginning.

"Again the names have not been changed."

"No, My Lord."

"There is something going on here," the Marquis said. "Something I do not like and it points unpleasantly to fraud."

"No, My Lord. That is not true, My Lord!"

Mr. Markham was now shaking and as if Anthony found

the interrogation too uncomfortable he got up and walked from the Library.

The Marquis brought his fist down suddenly on the desk so that the ink-pot rattled.

"I want the truth," he said angrily, "the whole truth!"

Mr. Markham drew in his breath.

At that moment from the open window a voice said:

"And that is what you shall have, My Lord!"

CHAPTER FIVE

The Marquis stared in astonishment as Ivana Wadebridge walked into the room.

She was wearing the emerald green gown in which he had first seen her and it made her look very picturesque besides accentuating her white skin.

As she came nearer he thought she looked unnaturally pale – in fact, frightened.

He was so astounded at her sudden appearance that he did not rise but remained sitting at his desk.

Then Markham who was standing in front of him exclaimed:

"No, no, Miss Ivana. Leave this to me. You must not be involved."

Ivana smiled at him.

"But I am involved, Marky, and we cannot go on pretending. His Lordship had better know the worst."

"No, please," Mr. Markham pleaded.

'Leave it to me," she said firmly, "and I prefer to speak to His Lordship alone."

Mr. Markham seemed about to go on protesting, then as if he felt helpless he merely made a gesture with his hands and went from the room.

As the door closed behind him, Ivana turned to face the Marquis standing in front of his desk as Mr Markham had done.

"You seem to have taken charge of my servants," the Marquis said in an icy voice, "but I am prepared, Mrs. Wadebridge, to listen to your explanation of what has been occurring here at Heathcliffe."

He looked down at the ledger as he spoke and then as he was aware that Ivana was feeling for words, he asked sharply:

"Why are you here in the first place? And why have you entered the house in such a strange manner?"

"I came to see Travers," she answered. "And I was told that you had taken the ledger from the Estate Office into the Library."

"You were – told?" the Marquis queried. "Does everything that happens here reach your ears?"

"A great deal of it."

The Marquis made an exasperated sound and sat back in his chair.

"I am listening," he said, "and, as I have already said to Markham, I want the truth."

Ivana gave a little sigh.

"I realised as soon as you arrived so unexpectedly that we could not go on as we were."

"It was obviously unfortunate that I decided to visit my own house," the Marquis said sarcastically.

'It was, as far as we were concerned."

"Who is 'We?'"

"Nanny, Marky, Travers, and of course the men we have been helping."

The Marquis's lips tightened, then he said

"I am waiting to hear about these men. I imagine they are sailors."

"Of course."

"Suppose you start at the beginning."

Then as if even in his anger he was aware he should be showing good manners, he said somewhat grudgingly:

"Do you wish to sit down?"

"No, thank you," Ivana replied. "I would rather stand. I am well aware, My Lord, that you are sitting in judgement upon me."

The Marquis did not reply.

His eyes were hard and he was thinking that although he

was curious to know how he had been tricked and made to look a fool of, by his servants, it was something he disliked intensely and to the offenders he intended to show no mercy.

As if she knew what he was thinking, Ivana said after a moment:

"I think perhaps as you said, I had best start at the beginning."

"I should have thought that was obvious," the Marquis said coldly.

"It all began three years ago when my brother Charles came back to England with his ship after the Battle of the Nile."

"In which your father was killed."

"Yes. Charles was a midshipman and he survived."

Ivana paused and the Marquis thought there was a suspicion of tears in her eyes, and there was certainly a throb in her voice as she went on:

"Charles told me how bravely Papa had died, and he also brought home with him a sailor who, he said, had saved his life, but who had afterwards been badly wounded."

Ivana paused a moment before she said:

"As I am sure Your Lordship is aware, nothing is done by a disgracefully ungrateful country for those who have been injured at sea. They are just dismissed and cast off as paupers to live on what they can beg or . . steal."

"I am aware of that," the Marquis replied, "and I consider it a scandal but there is nothing I can do about it."

"I thought that would be your attitude," Ivana said scornfully, "and that was why I felt justified . . ."

She stopped and said:

"I had better continue with my story."

"That is certainly advisable," the Marquis said, "rather than become side-tracked into recriminations which will get us nowhere."

He saw the flash of anger in Ivana's blue eyes before she went on:

"Nanny and I nursed George back to life, although he will always be a hopeless cripple."

"I suppose that is the man with the wooden leg?"

"So you did notice it!"

"I notice most things," he said.

"I was afraid you might be curious about it.'

"Only because you lied to me and said that you and your Nurse were alone in the house, although I suppose actually the man sleeps in the barn."

"Why should you think that?"

"Because I saw a light in the window after Sir Anthony and I had driven you home."

"That was careless," Ivana said, "but I could not have anticipated that you would accompany me."

"Of course not, but when one is telling lies one has to take every precaution against being found out."

The Marquis spoke scathingly, but Ivana went on:

"When George was a little better and Nanny and I were very proud of what we had been able to do for him, we went shopping in Brighton one day. I saw two other sailors there begging in the streets from the fashionable ladies and gentlemen parading themselves in their jewels along the Steine."

There was a contemptuous note in her voice as she went on:

"They were almost skin and bone, and anyone who was not blind could see they were half-starved. But nobody stopped to help them, no-one would give them a 4d. piece out of the hundreds of pounds which we are told are gambled away every night in the Royal Pavilion!"

"So you brought them back to Flagstaff House with you," the Marquis said.

"Of course I did! How could the people of this country leave men who have nearly died to keep us free from Bonaparte, in such a condition?"

As she spoke Ivana was almost spitting the words at him, but he said in a deliberately calm and indifferent voice:

"Continue with your story."

"I suppose the word got around of what had happened," she went on. "Anyway, more men came to ask our help and I could not .. turn them .. away."

She looked at the Marquis as if she appealed to him to understand, but he said after a moment:

"Then I imagine you ran out of money?"

Ivana nodded.

"I sold all the jewellery Mama had left me, and spent every penny of the small allowance I receive from Charles. I could not sell the furniture because that belongs to him."

"So instead you appealed to Markham to help you."

"He had always been a tremendous admirer of my father's and when Papa was killed he was almost as upset as I was. He knew I felt that in helping these sailors I was doing something of which Papa would have approved."

"So he began to 'cook the books'?" the Marquis said harshly.

"It was not exactly like that. As the footmen left one by one, he did not replace them. He handed over to me the money he received from you for their wages."

"And that was not enough?"

"We managed", Ivana replied, "until about a year ago. Then more and more men begged our help, and although I tried to be firm and send them away, I could not bear their helplessness, the manner in which they did not plead with me, but merely said:

" 'I understand, Ma'am, I'll manage somehow'."

Her voice broke and she said:

"I knew they could not manage, not with their wounds turning gangrenous. Some of them had lost an arm or a leg, some could not even think properly and were .. half-dazed from the .. horrors they had been .. through."

"So what did you do?" the Marquis asked, but he thought before Ivana replied, that he knew the answer.

"I sold a snuff-box."

There was silence while the Marquis stared at Ivana and she seemed incapable of continuing her story.

Then with an effort she said:

"It was not one of the best ones, in fact I thought it rather ugly. But the Dealer who had bought my mother's jewellery gave me a surprisingly large sum for it."

The Marquis remembered the box he had been shown by Peregrine Percival.

"But one was not enough. So you went on stealing."

"Y . yes," Ivana said. "Having taken one, and Marky had no idea I had done so .. I took another .. then another."

She made a helpless little gesture with her hands.

'They were not the best, they were the ones I thought, if you learnt about it, which seemed was very unlikely as you never came to Heathcliffe, you would miss the least."

"So you actually considered me in this extraordinarily reprehensible behaviour!" the Marquis said cynically.

"I knew how much they had meant to your father, because Marky told me. But as you had so many other interests over and above Heathcliffe, I did not think you would miss what you obviously did not value personally."

"That was a quite unwarranted presumption," the Marquis snapped.

"I realise that now, since you have been here and seem so interested in the pictures. But at the time I thought an absentee owner was less important than a war and the men who were fighting in it."

Ivana said this defiantly, and as her eyes met the Marquis's it was as if she battled with him.

"Go on," the Marquis ordered. "I am wondering where Bateman comes into this."

"Bateman resented being without footmen," Ivana replied, "and actually he was incapable of doing anything because having the keys to the cellar he just drank and drank until half the time he was in such a drunken stupor that he could not even move."

"Markham should have reported it to me," the Marquis said angrily.

"He wanted to, but I persuaded him not to," Ivana answered, "because we needed the money. Then I sent Travers here regularly to keep the place clean and tidy."

"Travers was with you?" the Marquis asked.

"Yes, he came to me from Charles. He was only slightly wounded, but it meant that he could not go back to his ship for six months, and before he was well enough to do so the peace came. Then I needed him desperately."

"Why?"

"Because, as you know, sailors were made redundant in their hundreds. I think it was worse on other parts of the coast, but there were too many here for me to cope with."

"What do you mean by that?" the Marquis asked.

"Most of the men had homes to go to or at least could return to their own towns where there was a chance of local assistance. But the trouble was, they had no money to get there."

"Are you telling me you supplied them with money for that purpose?"

"You can imagine what happened when they first came ashore," Ivana said. 'There were harpies, crooks and pick-pockets all waiting to take from them any wages they might have saved. After two nights on land, most of them were completely penniless."

"Surely that was their own fault?" the Marquis suggested.

Ivana just looked at him and he had a sudden vision of Lady Rose's face when he awoke after having too much to drink and found her beside him.

"Continue with what you were telling me," he said sharply.

"Travers sorted out for me the men who were really worth helping," Ivana said, "and we gave them enough money to get home and to buy food on the way. The ones that were scroungers he turned away, which I should never have been able to do on my own."

"So Travers was really *your* servant."

"Yes," Ivana admitted, "but when we heard you were returning I sent him quickly to Heathcliffe taking with him as footmen the four most able men we could find at a moment's notice."

The Marquis thought of the four clumsy lackeys in the ill-fitting livery and how Travers had seemed to do all the serving.

"I presume Travers was on your brother's ship," he said after a moment.

"He was the Admiral's personal servant."

'I might have guessed it!' the Marquis thought.

Aloud he said:

"Actually I was suspicious even before I arrived, that something was happening here. One of my guests at Veryan had a snuff-box that I was quite certain had been in my father's collection. It depicted a battleship on an emerald sea."

"I was afraid you might mind losing that when I sold it."

"Again I suppose I should be grateful that you even thought of me," the Marquis remarked, "and let me add that when I arrived and saw the cabinet was nearly empty, I was aware that a number of snuff-boxes were missing."

"I was hoping you would not notice that until after I had robbed you!"

The Marquis looked at her in astonishment.

"Good God!" he exclaimed. "So you were the Highwayman!"

Ivana nodded.

"It was the only way I thought I could prevent you from realising the snuff-boxes were not there."

"Then they were all that are left?" the Marquis enquired. "I thought perhaps some of them might have been put in the safe."

"I anticipated you might think that too," Ivana replied. "That is why I made one of the men come through the Pantry door."

"You certainly seem to think of everything. I could hardly believe that you could play the part of a man so well, although I did half suspect it after I heard you say you were a mimic."

"That was another mistake to call the parakeets," Ivana said with a sigh, "but you kept asking about the barn and I was so afraid that you might insist on looking inside."

"What would I have seen?" the Marquis asked.

"There are only five wounded men left," Ivana replied, "but that night there were ten others staying whom we were sending home to different parts of England the next day."

"You are certainly organising things on a grand scale with my money," the Marquis remarked.

"I am .. sorry, but I can give you back the snuff-boxes that are left and of course, your watch and the gold ship."

"Why, as a matter of interest, did you take that?"

"Because I thought you would think it strange if a Highwayman left anything so valuable behind on the table. But I promise you I would never have sold it. It belongs particularly to Heathcliffe as perhaps nothing else does."

"That sounds very convincing, Mrs. Wadebridge," the Marquis said sneeringly. "I am just wondering whether, if I had not returned now, there would soon have been any of my possessions left. What about the pictures and the furniture?"

"It is no use my trying to excuse myself," Ivana answered. "I am aware how angry this must make you, but I felt what I was doing was right and just."

"Just – for who?"

"For England!"

"I think your notions of justice are somewhat muddled, I might even say twisted," the Marquis said. "Or do you fancy yourself as a latter-day Robin Hood, stealing from the rich to give to the poor?"

He spoke so contemptuously that Ivana felt her anger rising.

"Perhaps it is a good comparison, My Lord," she replied,

"but to be truthful, it was stealing from the very, very rich for the men who were prepared to die so that his possessions should not be taken from him by the French."

The Marquis thought she had scored a point and he said:

"You can hardly expect me to approve of your methods however well you doll them up with pretty words."

"I have no wish to do that," Ivana said. "All I want is that you should understand that everything that has happened here was my fault and my fault entirely."

"Markham was my agent and as such his loyalty should have been to me as his employer."

"Is that all that matters to you?" Ivana asked. "He had a deep affection for my father and, though he connived at giving the sailors the money, you were paying for servants who were doing nothing, he did not know for a long time that I was stealing from you."

"And when he did?" the Marquis enquired.

"He was shocked .. very shocked, but when he saw the suffering of the men I was trying to help, he knew that without extra money for medicines and the food they required they would soon join those we .. had buried in the .. Churchyard."

There was a quiver in Ivana's voice as she said:

"Four died last year and three the year before. Nanny and I did everything we could, but it was hopeless .. they were .. all so .. badly hurt."

The Marquis looked down at the ledger.

"You have made out a good case for yourself, Mrs. Wadebridge," he said, "but I am certainly not happy about the way Markham has behaved in this whole matter."

"I have explained to you ..."

"I know," the Marquis interrupted, "but, as I have said, Markham is my agent. I trusted him and he has abused that trust, which is something I will not tolerate."

Ivana gave a little cry and moved nearer the desk.

"You cannot mean ...?" she said. "You cannot .. intend to .. dismiss him?"

"I see no other course of action."

"But you must not do that! He has been here all these years. It is his life. He loves Heathcliffe. He would die for .. the house and .. your family."

"All I ask is that he should live honestly while he is working for me."

"You cannot be so .. cruel .. so hard," Ivana said. "It would .. kill him to go .. away. Besides .. where would he go? He has no .. money saved."

"I suppose you spent that too."

"I tried to prevent him from being so generous, but he insisted and would often give the men .. something behind my .. back."

"That was his decision," the Marquis said.

Ivana looked at him and thought that his expression was merciless.

"How can I plead with you?" she asked. "What can I say to make you .. understand that Marky must not .. suffer for this?"

Her hands were on the desk now as she said:

"Listen to me .. My Lord. Please .. listen."

The Marquis's eyes were on her face as she went on:

"I will do .. anything you tell me to do. You can .. punish me in any .. way you wish .. even send me to prison and I will not .. complain. But do not make Marky .. suffer for .. my sins."

"Your sins are a very different matter, Mrs. Wadebridge," the Marquis said, "and as you have said yourself, the punishment for your crime is very obvious."

Ivana stiffened but she did not speak.

"You mean .. prison!"

"You must be aware that anyone who steals above the value of one shilling is liable to be hanged?"

Ivana did not move or speak. Only her eyes widened until they seemed to fill her whole face.

"Is that what you .. intend shall .. happen to .. me?" she whispered after a moment's silence.

The Marquis did not reply and she said proudly:

"I have no defence. All I can ask is that if I die you will .. exonerate Marky from his part in what I have done and look after my old Nurse .. because she too has .. spent her .. life-savings."

"Can you think of any reason why I should do these things?" the Marquis asked, "after the way you have treated me?"

"Does it mean nothing to you that you have been instrumental in saving the lives of at least fifty men who would otherwise have died, and preventing a much larger number of others from turning to a life of crime?"

"You are very plausible in your own defence."

"I have already told you I am not thinking of myself," Ivana retorted. "But if you will save Marky I will do any-thing .. anything you ask of me."

"Anything?" the Marquis enquired with a twist of his lips.

"I swear to you that is true by .. everything I hold .. sacred."

"Very well . . ." the Marquis began.

He would have said more, but at that moment the door of the Library opened and Anthony came into the room.

"Look out, Justin!" he said in a low, warning voice.

Than as the Marquis looked at him with astonishment behind him came a vision in the shape of Lady Rose.

She was wearing one of the new muslins which Ladies of Fashion dampened so that it clung to their figures and made it appear as if they were partially naked.

As if to compensate for her body being so lightly clad Lady Rose wore on her head a bonnet with a large turned-up brim and a high crown that was massed with pink ostrich feathers.

Round her throat was a necklace of turquoises and dia-monds while the same stones glittered beneath her fair hair in her shell-like ears.

She looked sensational and breathtakingly beautiful.

She stood for a moment in the doorway as if to give the

Marquis the chance of admiring her. Then with a little cry of joy she ran towards him.

"Justin, dearest! I have found you!" she exclaimed. "How could you leave in that unkind and cruel fashion? I have been distraught, absolutely distraught, wondering where you could be, then . . ."

"I told her where you could be hiding," a deep, plummy voice announced, and following her into the room came the Prince of Wales!

He was obviously in one of his merry good humours.

Ivana who had never seen him before, stared with undisguised interest at his laughing eyes and pouting lips.

He was tall but over-fat, his clothes fitted him like a glove, and around his throat was a huge white cravat with many folds out of which she thought his chin seemed almost to be struggling to emerge.

The whole impression he gave was one of stylish elegance, and he had an unmistakable presence which told her that even in a crowd she would have known that he was of Royal blood.

The Marquis, who had risen automatically to his feet as Lady Rose spoke to him, now moved forward hastily to bow and take the hand the Prince held out to him.

"This is a great surprise, Sire!"

"I thought it would be," the Prince said with a chuckle. "But when Lady Rose cried on my shoulder and said she could not find you, I guessed where you had run to earth."

"You were right, Sire," the Marquis said.

"And Justin," Lady Rose cried, as if determined to keep herself in the picture, "I have told His Royal Highness our little secret."

The Marquis stiffened.

"Secret?" he enquired.

"Of course, dearest. I knew you would wish to tell him yourself, but it just slipped out when I was so unhappy."

"I must congratulate you, Justin," the Prince said,

"congratulate you most sincerely. You will have the loveliest wife in England, just as you have the finest horses."

For a moment the Marquis seemed stunned. Then he knew with a sudden fury that seemed to rise up inside him like an explosive bomb, that he had been tricked.

Rose had won! Rose had him exactly where she wanted him, and there was nothing he could do about it.

He thought despairingly that he was cornered, caught, captured, snared by a woman who had been cleverer than he was.

Then a movement behind him made him remember Ivana.

He realised that she was tactfully backing away towards the window, obviously intending to leave as she had arrived.

It was then an idea came to him; an idea that seemed to follow naturally on the last words she had spoken when she had sworn a sacred oath that she would do anything – anything he asked of her.

There was a note in his voice which Anthony thought sounded like one of triumph as he said:

"One minute! I fear there has been some mistake, and I cannot imagine quite how it has occurred."

"Mistake?" Lady Rose asked.

Now there was a wary look in her eyes, which told the Marquis, if he had not known it before, that all her effusiveness had been well planned so that he should be aware that he was trapped and there was no escape.

"Yes, indeed," the Marquis said.

He walked towards Ivana and took her by the hand, pulling her forward so that they stood side by side in front of the Prince.

"May I, Sire," he asked, "present my wife who was the daughter of Captain Wadebridge who died a hero's death at the Battle of the Nile."

As the Marquis spoke he tightened his fingers on Ivana's hand, telling her without words what he asked of her.

Just for a moment it seemed as if everybody in the room

was frozen into immobility. Then the Prince of Wales with a laugh exclaimed:

"You always manage to surprise me, Justin! It is one of the things I most enjoy about you. I never guessed, I never anticipated for one moment that you might spring a secret marriage on me! But of course, I congratulate you, and wish your bride every possible happiness."

He took Ivana's hand as she rose from a deep curtsey and as he looked at her, he said:

"Now I see you, I understand how the elusive Marquis has been persuaded to relinquish his heart into your keeping."

The Prince with a grace and charm that had always proved irresistible, raised Ivana's hand to his lips.

As he did so, Lady Rose seemed to break the inertia which had held her spellbound.

"I do not believe it! It is impossible!" she said to the Marquis. "How can you have married in such a short time, without anybody being aware of it?"

"My best friend was with me," the Marquis said, a smile on his lips as he indicated Anthony.

As he spoke he saw that Lady Rose was looking searchingly at Ivana's hand.

She saw the wedding-ring and drew in her breath with what was almost a hiss.

"I will never forgive you for this, Justin!" she said. "Never! And one day I will get even with you!"

As if Anthony realised he must do something, he moved to her side.

"Come into the garden, Rose," he said. "I want to talk to you."

He drew her firmly towards the window as he spoke and she went with him reluctantly. Then they heard her voice, high and fretful, as Anthony escorted her from the terrace onto the lawn.

"May I offer you some refreshment, Sire?" the Marquis asked.

"I could certainly do with a glass of champagne after all these dramatics," the Prince replied. "At least, Justin, things are never monotonous when you are about."

Before the Marquis could ring the bell for Travers he appeared as if anticipating what would be required with trays containing glasses and other wines should they be preferred.

In an extremely genial mood, the Prince seated himself on the sofa and insisted on Ivana sitting beside him.

"Now tell me all about yourself, my dear," he said, "for I know Mrs. Fitzherbert will want to know everything about your marriage to one of my dearest friends."

"It is such a privilege to meet Your Royal Highness," Ivana replied, "that I find it difficult to think of anything else."

The Prince was delighted, for if there was one thing he really enjoyed it was being flattered by a pretty woman.

"We cannot have met before otherwise I know I should have remembered you," he said.

"I have heard so much about you, Sire, because I have always lived so near to Brighton," Ivana said, "and I know how much you have done to make the town fashionable, and how everyone talks of the wonder and beauty of the Royal Pavilion."

"Not everyone is as pleased with it as I am myself," the Prince said, "but make Justin bring you to see it as soon as you have finished your honeymoon."

"That is extremely kind of you, Sire," the Marquis said, "but I think we would be wise to wait until Lady Rose has left Brighton."

The Prince threw back his head and laughed.

"You certainly gave her a shock. It was my fault for telling her where you could be hiding."

He chuckled before he said:

"To tell the truth, Justin, it was only after I had been indiscreet enough to reveal that you had a house here, that it occurred to me that the one person you did not wish to find you was Rose Caterham."

"That was very perceptive of you, Sire," the Marquis replied dryly.

"She was so insistent that you were engaged," the Prince went on as if he wished to excuse himself, "and now I am not looking forward to the journey back."

"I am sorry, Sire," the Marquis said, "but if it had been possible I would have taken you into my confidence."

"That is what I would have wished you to do."

"I feel, Sire, that with your usual tact and diplomacy which are unequalled," the Marquis said, "you will be able to smooth things over one way or another, and I can tell you in all truth, that I never had any intention whatever of marrying Lady Rose."

The Prince always enjoyed being taken into anyone's confidence, especially when it was somebody like the Marquis who he always considered was rather tight-lipped where his love-affairs were concerned.

"Leave it to me, dear fellow," he said. "I will make everything right for you."

"I knew I could rely on you, Sire," the Marquis said in a heart-felt tone which sounded so sincere that it would have made Anthony smile if he had been present.

The Prince accepted another glass of champagne, then rose to his feet.

"I must be getting back," he said. "Mrs. Fitzherbert will be waiting for me. As you know, there is only room in my Phaeton for two."

That was certainly true of anybody as fat as His Royal Highness.

The Marquis, glad to be rid of them, hurried to the terrace to beckon to Anthony who was listening to a long monologue from an infuriated Lady Rose.

They came back quickly onto the terrace and Lady Rose walked past the Marquis with her head high and without speaking.

They joined the Prince in the Library who was already on his feet admiring one of the ship-pictures on the wall with Ivana beside him.

"Your wife has been explaining to me one of the battles in which her ancestors took part," the Prince said to the Marquis. "It is very interesting, very interesting indeed. I am anxious to show her some of the Naval trophies I have at the Royal Pavilion."

"It will be an honour, Sire," the Marquis said.

"And I hope you will invite me over here again," the Prince remarked, "perhaps one day next week or the week after, I could bring Mrs. Fitzherbert over?"

"We should be delighted to receive Your Royal Highness!" the Marquis declared.

The Prince put out his hand to Ivana.

"My very best wishes for your future happiness," he said, "and make no mistake, you are the prettiest Marchioness of the Veryans. Your husband must decide who would be the best artist to paint you, so that your portrait will hang in the Picture Gallery amongst his ancestors."

He kissed Ivana's hand and the Marquis said:

"I was going to ask Your Royal Highness's advice on that very subject just as soon as I had the opportunity."

Lady Rose had already stalked out of the Library.

Now the Prince followed with the Marquis beside him, discussing as he went, the merits of the different portrait-painters on whom he was an acknowledged expert.

Anthony stayed behind for a second to say to Ivana in a low voice: "Well done!" before he followed the Prince and the Marquis into the Hall.

She stood for a moment staring after them, then she put her hands up to her face.

It seemed almost incredible that so much had happened in such a very short space of time: she had confronted the Marquis; he had threatened her with being hanged for the theft of his possessions; then with the arrival of the most fantastically beautiful woman she had ever seen in her life, she had apparently saved him from an unwelcome engagement.

It seemed extraordinary to Ivana that anyone could not wish to marry a woman as beautiful as Lady Rose.

At the same time, she did not miss the spiteful manner in which she had spoken to the Marquis or the way in which she had ignored him when she left.

He had extricated himself from a very difficult situation only by lying and she wondered what he intended to do in the future, when he would be required to produce a wife who did not, in fact, exist.

She thought the best thing she could do would be to go back to Flagstaff House.

She was still desperately afraid that he might dismiss Mr. Markham as he had said he would. Then she told herself that however incensed he might be with her, she had at least done Marky a good turn.

She could not believe in the circumstances they were in at the moment, he would be so unjust as to dismiss his agent before discussing it with her further.

"But we cannot go on arguing about it now,' she thought in a sudden panic.

Thinking she heard voices returning to the Library, she ran through the open window back towards the stables, where she had left the pony-trap in which she had journeyed to Heathcliffe.

. . . .

The Marquis was not as it happened, very surprised when he came back into the Library to find Ivana gone. He had anticipated that she would run away.

He walked to where the drinks had been put down on a side-table and poured himself a glass of champagne.

Anthony followed him into the room and shut the door behind him.

"What the devil is all this about?" he asked. "I realise you have saved yourself at Ivana's expense, but what was she doing here in the first place?"

"She came to explain to me what had been going on," the Marquis said, a note of satisfaction in his voice, "and I now know the whole story! It might be a melodrama straight from Drury Lane."

Anthony helped himself to a glass of champagne.

"If you had listened to the way Rose was ranting, you would be wary of every dark corner for fear of a dagger in your back!" he said.

"I thought I was extremely clever to escape the trap she set for me," the Marquis replied. "For one moment I thought I was doomed!"

"I thought the same thing," Anthony said. "But what is Ivana going to say? It must have been more than a surprise to her!"

"She had sworn to do anything I asked of her," the Marquis replied, "to save Markham from being dismissed."

"You are not telling that I owe you fifty guineas?" Anthony enquired.

"I certainly am," the Marquis replied. "She was the Highwayman, and she had stolen the snuff-boxes long before the night we arrived, and only held us up to ransom so that she could save Markham from the dire consequences of his collaboration with her."

"If you think I understand a word of that," Anthony said, "you can start again from the beginning."

The Marquis sat down, his glass in his hand, and told Anthony exactly what Ivana had told him.

As he finished Anthony said:

"It is the finest and most magnificent thing I have ever heard in my life! She ought to get a medal for what she has done, and it certainly ought to show up the Government for the criminal manner in which they are treating our wounded."

"That is all very well," the Marquis remarked, "but the person who has paid for all this generosity is me!"

"You can well afford it! Heavens – what a woman she is! Can you imagine Rose or Lucy or any of the other frivolous idiots we know caring a damn for men starving on the door-step or bleeding from a gun-shot wound?"

He laughed as he added:

"If they so much as prick a finger they swoon at the sight of blood! I hope, Justin, you told Ivana how much you admired her."

"I told her I was considering whether I would have her hanged!"

"What did you say?" Anthony exclaimed. Then added: "I know you are joking!"

"No. That is what I actually said."

"Why?"

"I thought it would do her no harm to be a little fright-ened of the consequences of her actions."

"Do you mean to tell me you let her go home thinking you might have her strung from a gibbet or taken to Tyburn Hill?"

"We had not really finished our conversation."

"Then the sooner you go to Flagstaff House and do so, the better!"

"Wait a minute! the Marquis said. "You are moving too fast. We have both been made to look stupid fools by women, especially by Ivana. Does that mean nothing to you?"

"It is not a story with which I wish to regale the Prince of Wales or tell at White's," Anthony replied. "All I can say is that Wadebridge is fortunate enough to have a wife in a million."

There was silence. Then the Marquis said:

"Of course – Wadebridge! I had forgotten about him!"

CHAPTER SIX

As the Marquis spoke Travers came into the room with the newspapers.

He put them down on the long tapestry-covered stool by the hearth-rug and Anthony immediately picked up 'The Times'.

As Travers left the room shutting the door behind him, the Marquis said: "There is something I want to see Travers about," and followed him.

He caught up with the man just before he reached the Hall.

"When Mrs. Wadebridge was here a short time ago," he said, "she told me she had come to see you about something that was troubling her. What was it?"

"I was intending to ask Your Lordship," Travers replied, "if I could slip down to Flagstaff House for a short while. I thinks there's a bit of trouble brewing."

"Trouble?" the Marquis enquired. "What sort of trouble?"

"Mrs. Wadebridge tells me, M'Lord, that Nurse has reported seeing a man lurking in the bushes and peering at the house."

"Why should he be doing that?" the Marquis asked.

"There're a lot of ruffians about at the moment with so many men being demobilised, M'Lord, and Nurse thought he might be intending to rob them."

The Marquis frowned.

"I will see to it," he said after a moment. "I wish to speak to Mrs. Wadebridge anyway."

He was just about to return to the Libarary to tell Anthony where he was going when it struck him that Anthony would certainly commend Ivana for her actions while he intended to be extremely critical of them.

Looking through the open front door he could see in charge of two grooms, the horses which, since the Prince of Wales' arrival he had forgotten that he had ordered.

He walked towards them saying over his shoulder to Travers:

"Tell Sir Anthony I will not be long."

Swinging himself into the saddle of a fine stallion he set off across the grass towards Flagstaff House.

As he went the full impact of what he had done in introducing Ivana Wadebridge as his wife really struck him. He realised that he had got himself out of one tangle and into another.

He was well aware that the news that he had been married would be known within a few hours by the whole of fashionable Brighton.

The Prince of Wales always wished to play the lead in anything that was likely to cause a sensation, and what could be more sensational than that one of his closest friends, and certainly one of the most important figures in the Social World, had been married secretly to a woman of whom none of them had ever heard?

He was quite sure that the Prince would extol Ivana's beauty if only to pique Lady Rose, and there would be a great number of women who would be delighted to see the latter take a set-back.

Her success in monopolising many of the most eligible and attractive bachelors had made her a lot of enemies.

The Marquis now admitted to himself that while he was delighted to be rid of Rose Caterham he had, in fact, tumbled out of the frying-pan into the fire.

For almost the first time he asked himself what attitude Ivana would take. He presumed that he owed her some sort of apology even though she might accept his behaviour as a just retribution for the manner in which she had deceived and tricked him.

"What am I to do?" he asked himself over and over again, as he galloped his horse, as if by moving very quickly he could run away from his problems.

He had come to no solution by the time he reached Flagstaff House. In fact, the difficulties ahead seemed even worse than they had when he started.

It was the question not only of his feelings and Ivana's but of her husband's. When he returned home Mr. Wadebridge might have some very strong views about his wife being talked of as the wife of another man.

The Marquis felt as if a number of unanswerable questions were hammering at his brain.

As he dismounted outside the front door of Flagstaff House, he told himself that the only possible thing to do was to talk it over sensibly and quietly with Ivana and see if she had any solution.

This afternoon there was no groom to take his horse, and he therefore tied the reins of the stallion to the branch of a tree hoping that the animal would not become entangled.

The horse however, put his head down and started to crop the grass and the Marquis thought he would be all right.

Then he walked to the front door and seeing it open did not bother to knock as he had done before, but walked in.

There appeared to be nobody about, but the staircase and furniture seemed even more highly polished than before and the scent of bees'-wax mingled with the fragrance of the flowers which had been skilfully arranged in a large bowl on one of the hall-tables.

It struck him that Ivana besides her other unusual activities was skilful at making her home attractive.

Then as he thought of her, he heard voices from a room which she had told him was her father's Study.

He walked towards it, opened the door, then was still with surprise at what he saw.

Ivana was standing behind her father's desk and opposite

126

her in a threatening attitude with a knife in his hand stood a large, unpleasant-looking man in a tattered sailor's uniform.

. . . .

Driving back from Heathcliffe behind the fat, slow pony that was too old to be hurried Ivana felt that she had stepped into a strange, night-marish drama from which she could not awaken.

She could hardly believe that the Marquis had actually threatened to see her hanged because she had stolen his possessions and that Marky, after thirty-five years in the service of the Veryans, might be dismissed.

Even more incredible was the fact that she had been introduced to the Prince of Wales by the Marquis as his wife, and she had been unable to do or say anything to contradict such an absurd statement.

"What will happen now?" she asked herself. "How can he possibly explain away something which seemed so convincing that the Prince actually believed it?"

It seemed extraordinary that the Marquis had no wish to marry anyone so beautiful as Lady Rose, but even so, to contradict her assertion that they were engaged by producing a wife as it were, out of thin air, was Ivana thought, too fantastic for her even to be sure it had actually happened.

If that was the unaccountable way Society behaved, then she was glad she was not part of it.

Nevertheless for the moment she was involved because the Marquis would have to announce sooner or later that she was not his wife, and what explanation could he produce for being rid of her?

Then it struck Ivana that she was so unimportant and insignificant that she would just be able to disappear and no further explanations would be necessary.

"I suppose I could be drowned at sea, or die of some

obscure disease, and he need not even feel obliged to mourn for me," she thought.

At least, she told herself, she had been able to render him a service which should make him more inclined to be merciful to Marky and perhaps to her than he had been before Lady Rose's arrival.

"Maybe the whole thing will turn out to be a blessing in disguise," she told herself with a rising of her spirits.

At the same time, she thought uncomfortably that the Marquis was very formidable.

She had known when she faced him across his desk that he was extremely angry, even though he controlled his feelings to speak in a sarcastic, contemptuous voice which made her feel almost as if he hit her.

"How could I have done anything so foolish as to rob somebody as frightening as the Marquis?" she asked herself, and remembered she had had no alternative.

As she had said to him, it was either a question of selling the snuff-boxes or letting men die whom she knew, with enough money to feed and treat them, Nanny and she could save.

'We have not been extravagant,' she thought piteously, 'we have skimped and saved on ourselves. But men need a lot of food, and there were other things that proved expensive.'

She was thinking of the fares for which she had to find the money.

There was one sailor who came from Northumberland, another from Cornwall, and however cheaply they travelled on the outside of stage-coaches, each man required a number of guineas if he was to reach his destination.

Woman-like, she could not help for a moment being aware of the difference between her appearance and that of Lady Rose.

She had known before she saw the slim, revealing muslin that barely seemed to cover the beauty's nakedness, that her own gown was lamentably out of fashion.

And the bonnet with its up-turned brim reaching almost to a point high over her lovely face was smarter and different from the bonnets the ladies had been wearing when Ivana last visited Brighton.

Her turquoises and diamonds glittering in the sunshine which came through the windows of the Library had, Ivana was sure, cost an astronomical amount of money.

She was not envious, she was merely aware of the contrast between herself and the woman who personified the Fashionable World in which the Marquis moved.

"How could anyone for a single moment think I was his wife?" Ivana said to herself.

She found herself wondering what the Marquis had said to Lady Rose to make her think that he intended to marry her.

Had he kissed her? She was sure that if he had done so he would kiss with an elegance and an expertise which was characteristic of everything else he did.

Ivana had not missed the way he sat a horse or how outstanding he looked when he was driving his Phaeton.

"He is the most handsome man I could ever imagine," she murmured.

She could understand why Lady Rose wanted to marry him and what a blow it must have been to be told that he was already wed to some 'country bumpkin' like herself.

'Perhaps one day I shall fall in love with somebody like the Marquis,' she thought, as the pony plodded on, making heavy weather of even the slightest incline and paying no attention when Ivana slapped the reins up and down in an effort to hurry him.

Then she had the uncomfortable feeling that now she had seen the Marquis any other man she might meet, would pale into insignificance.

She had always imagined that the heroes she read about in books and the man of her dreams who would one day be her husband would be wearing Naval uniform and have fair hair and the far-seeing eyes of men who were constantly looking at the sea.

But now, instead, he seemed to be wearing a tall hat at a raffish angle on the side of his dark head, and either a grey whip-cord or a superfine evening-coat which fitted over his athletic shoulders without a wrinkle.

Then she remembered the anger in the Marquis's voice and the steely expression in his eyes and felt herself tremble.

"He will never forgive me, not only for stealing his possessions but for involving his household in the theft," she told herself and her spirits sank to a new level.

She drove straight into the stables of Flagstaff House and because now there was no Travers to help her, she unharnessed the old pony, put him in his stall and saw there was plenty of hay in the manger.

Then she walked into the house.

It was very hot and she was almost certain that Nanny, having been up early first to tend their invalids, then later to give them their midday meal, was having a rest.

She was getting on in years and so much work made her tire easily. The only way she kept going was when the wounded men recovered enough to help in the house as well as in the garden.

When they were able-bodied they were of inestimable help for as long as they stayed.

As the Marquis had supposed, the tidiness of the garden was due to men who were so grateful for what had been done for them that they wished to do something in return.

Even those who were crippled, polished the stairs as they sat on them, cleaned the brasses and helped Nanny in the kitchen by peeling potatoes and shelling peas.

There were only five wounded men left at the moment and Ivana had told them firmly that they were to stay in the barn unless either she or Nanny told them it was safe for them to go outside into the court-yard.

When she had left Flagstaff House she had not known that the Marquis had discovered her secret, and she had been afraid that he or Sir Anthony might call unexpectedly to visit her and see the men in the garden.

She stopped for a moment in the hall to tidy her hair in front of a very old mirror, thinking as she did so, that the Marquis must have thought it strange that she was not wearing a bonnet.

She had never for a moment expected to see him when she had gone to Heathcliffe, thinking that he and Sir Anthony would be out riding or driving and she had taken the precaution of going to the back-door to ask for Travers.

When one of the footmen fetched him she saw at once by the expression on his face, that something was wrong.

"What is it?" she had asked.

"His Lordship's taken the ledger from the Estate Office into the Library, Miss Ivana, and has sent for Mr. Markham!"

Ivana had given a little gasp for she knew only too well what this portended.

Then she said:

"I expect the Library windows are open. I will go along the terrace and see if I can hear what is happening."

'It was a good thing I did so,' she thought now defiantly, 'otherwise the Marquis would have gone on bullying poor Marky, and frightening him into a fit!'

The idea made her angry, and she opened the door of the Study to walk in with a little flounce of her unfashionably full skirt.

Then as she reached the centre of the room she gave a scream.

The door closed behind her and she saw that hiding behind it had been a man!

One glance at his torn uniform that was almost in rags told her that he was a sailor and obviously one who had been discharged.

There was however, something about him which she disliked at first glance.

It was not only that he was dirty and unshaven, it was the expression in his eyes that told her immediately he was not one of the men who accepted almost fatalistically the fact that they were redundant.

"What are you doing here?" Ivana asked.

"Th' door were open," the man replied in a rough voice.

"If you had knocked I dare say someone would have answered it."

"Shut it in me fice more like!"

Ivana sat down at the desk.

"I suppose you have been told that I try to help sailors who have been made redundant from the ships that are being laid up," she said quietly, "but as you must understand, we cannot help everybody."

She had an idea as she spoke, that the man had not heard of her activities before but had merely been waiting for an opportunity to break into the house and steal anything that was of value.

She was too wise to say so however and she merely asked:

"What is your name?"

"Wot's that got ter do wi' ye?"

"I am trying to help you and I would obviously like some particulars. In some cases I can arrange for a man to travel back to his home, so suppose you tell me where you live?"

"Oi lives where Oi loiks," the man said coming up to the desk to face her. "Oi wants all t'money ye've got in t'house, an' any jools ye moight 'ave."

"In that case I am afraid you are going to be disappointed," Ivana replied. "I have no jewellery and the very little money I own, as I have already said, is to help sailors reach their homes, or perhaps take them to a town where they can obtain work."

"Oi've 'ad enough o' work ter last Oi a life-time!" the man said abruptly. "Nah, 'and over t'money, an' stop talkin' so much!"

As he spoke he pulled a knife from his belt and held it in his right hand pointing it towards Ivana.

"You are making a great mistake," she said calmly, although her heart was beating fast. "There are a number of sailors here at the moment and I have only to call out and they will come to my assistance."

"Make one sound," the man facing her said, "an' yer face won't look so pretty as it does nah!"

Instinctively Ivana rose to her feet and he gave an unpleasant laugh.

"If yer thinkin' o' runnin', yer won't get far. Oi'm sharp on me feet, as sharp as this 'ere knife!"

Ivana felt her heart thumping against her breast and her lips were suddenly dry.

She knew she was frightened, very frightened.

She remembered that the snuff-boxes she had taken from the Marquis were all locked in the centre drawer of the desk with the few sovereigns she had left over from the last sale which had actually been nearly a month ago.

She had been deciding she must sell yet another box from the Marquis's collection when he had arrived home unexpectedly.

Desperately she wondered what she should do.

If she opened the drawer to give the man the money she knew he would not miss what else the drawer contained.

As if he was aware she was hiding something from him, he became more aggressive.

"Ye'll 'urry up if ye knows wot's good fer yer," he said. "This knife'll slice through yer skin as if Oi was cuttin' butter! Come on, nah."

As Ivana thought despairingly there was nothing she could do but obey him, there was a footstep at the open door and there stood the Marquis!

For a moment everyone was still, then with a swiftness that afterwards seemed incredible the Marquis not only took in at a glance exactly what was happening, but acted.

He moved forward, raised his long, wiry riding-whip and brought it down with all his strength on the sailor's hand which held the knife.

The man gave a yell, the knife clattered to the floor and

the Marquis hit him under the chin with an upper-cut which swept him off his feet.

He staggered, crashed down on the floor unconscious and out for the count.

Then as the Marquis stood looking at him, a faint smile on his lips, Ivana flung herself at him and hid her face against his shoulder.

"T . thank God . . you came!" she said incoherently, her voice breaking as she went on: "I was . . f . frightened . . and the . . only . . m . money I have . . was in the . . drawer with your . . snuff-boxes."

The Marquis's arms went round her and as she trembled he thought how slim and frail she was.

"You really worried about my snuff-boxes with that unpleasant-looking customer holding a knife to your throat?"

'He was . . hiding b . behind the . . d . door," Ivana murmured.

The Marquis knew how frightened she had been.

"It is all over now," he said. "You are lucky this sort of thing has not happened before."

"The . . wounded men would . . never have . . frightened me," she answered, "and since the . . others have been . . demobilised I have had . . Travers."

"I suppose really I should apologise for taking him from you," the Marquis said.

There was just a touch of amusement in his voice which made Ivana realise the position she was in.

As if she suddenly became aware of the Marquis she moved from the shelter of his arms to say:

"W . what are we to d . do with . . this man?"

"Is there anybody else here capable of giving me a hand?" the Marquis enquired.

"George can do . . that," Ivana replied. "He is very . . strong although he . . only has one . . leg."

"Then let us go and find George," the Marquis said. "I suppose he is in the barn?"

Ivana nodded and he realised she was still finding it hard to speak.

As if he knew she did not wish to be left alone, he put out his hand saying:

"We will go and find him together."

Because she was still very pale and shaken by what had happened Ivana took his hand almost gratefully.

Her small fingers fluttered in his and the Marquis found himself thinking that she was not, after all, the aggressive woman who had held him up as a Highwayman, deliberately stolen his possessions and cheated him of his servants' wages.

She was little more than a child who had been frightened by brute strength and a knife which might easily have killed her.

He told himself this sort of thing must not happen again.

As they walked hand-in-hand across the court-yard towards the door of the barn, he decided the first thing he must do was to send for Travers to take charge at Flagstaff House.

Then he thought, the man who had arrived might not be the only desperado ready to cause trouble not only here, but in other parts of the neighbourhood.

For the second time that day it struck him that the Government's action in dismissing enormous numbers of men and throwing them onto the countryside without work and without money, might have serious repercussions.

They reached the barn and Ivana opened the door.

As he walked in the Marquis found himself staring in amazement at what had been happening in the huge, centuries-old Tithe Barn which had once held tons of grain.

At Harvest-time it had seen the labourers enjoying the festival dinner to which they looked forward all the year.

Now there were a number of mattresses on the floor and as if to accommodate extra men in an emergency, there were hammocks strung from the ships' beams which crossed the barn roof a few feet above a man's head.

At the far end of the barn there were three men lying on mattresses and two others sitting in chairs talking to them.

They all had bandages on some part of their anatomy and as Ivana walked towards them the Marquis saw their faces light up with pleasure.

"This is the Marquis of Veryan," Ivana said as she reached them, "and he has just knocked unconscious a very unpleasant man who was threatening me with a knife."

"Threatening ye, Miss?" one of the sailors asked.

"He wanted to steal all the money I had in the house."

"Ye should've called fer us, Miss," another said. "We'd 've soon dealt wi' a feller like that!"

"I want you to come and deal with him now," the Marquis intervened. "I do not wish to prosecute him, but to be rid of him all together. I think the best thing would be if we dragged him outside the gates and left him beside the roadway."

George the man with the wooden leg, stood up.

"Oi can manage that, M'Lord," he said, "wi' the 'elp o' Tim 'ere. 'E's got one sound arm that's worth two o' any other man's."

Tim grinned sheepishly at the praise and he too rose to his feet.

"Come along then," the Marquis said. "Let us get him outside before he comes round and gets abusive."

He smiled at Ivana as he said:

"Give us five minutes before you come back to the house. I am sure these gentlemen will take care of you in the meantime."

He walked away followed by George and Tim, and Ivana watched them until the door of the barn closed behind them.

It was over five minutes before George and Tim came back looking flushed and hot, but obviously very pleased with themselves.

"Us dragged 'im a good way, Miss," George said to Ivana. "An' shoved 'im in a ditch. Right place fer 'im Oi says."

"He is still unconscious?" Ivana enquired.

"Out like a light!" George replied, "and 'e'll find every tooth in 'is 'ead loose when 'e does come round!"

The other men wanted to know exactly how the Marquis had hit him but Ivana walked away and went back to the house.

As she expected, the Marquis was waiting for her in the Drawing-Room.

As she entered the room her eyes met his and she felt for one strange moment as if they were speaking to each other without words.

Then she said quickly in a shy little voice:

"H . how .. can I thank you? If you had .. not come .. when you did .."

"Forget it!" the Marquis interrupted. "But it is something which must not happen again. I have been thinking of what is the best thing to do."

"You cannot .. spare Travers, the footmen I sent with him have no experience and you would only be uncomfortable."

"My comforts take second place to your safety, Mrs. Wadebridge."

Ivana hesitated for a moment, then she said:

"There is .. no need for you to .. concern yourself with .. me. I know you must be thinking it is .. entirely my own fault that all this has happened. I suppose after .. Papa died I should not have .. stayed here alone .. with Nanny .. but there seemed nothing else I could do at the time .. and I could not bear to close up my .. home .. and live with relatives."

"I can understand that," the Marquis said, "but are you not forgetting somebody who should have looked after you and made the decision for you?"

"Who is that?" Ivana asked in surprise.

"Your husband!"

Ivana's eye-lids fluttered and he saw the colour rise in a crimson flood up her pale cheeks.

"Yes .. yes, of course," she said after a moment's silence, "but .. he was .. at sea."

The Marquis seated himself in a chair beside the fire-place.

"I am very interested in your husband," he said. "Tell me about him."

"There .. is nothing to .. tell."

"When were you married?"

"T . two .. years ago."

"Where?"

"Here in the .. village."

"You are quite certain of that? After all, it will be very easy to see a record of the ceremony in the Church Register."

There was silence, then Ivana asked:

"Why .. why should you be .. interested?"

"I am very interested," the Marquis said, "because ever since we have known each other, you have behaved in a very unpredictable fashion, and it is certainly something I did not expect when I came to Heathcliffe for peace and quiet."

She did not reply. He gave a little laugh and went on:

"Both of which have been distinctly missing! First of all I am held up by a Highwayman, then I discover I have been robbed by my nearest neighbour, thirdly I have to save her from what might have been a very unpleasant assault if I had not turned up in the nick of time."

"I .. I am trying to .. thank you," Ivana said, "but I suppose it puts me even more .. heavily in your debt than .. I am already."

"I have thought of that," the Marquis replied. "At the same time, I have not forgotten that you have helped me out of a very uncomfortable situation."

"I was wondering as I drove back here," Ivana said, "how you would go about getting rid of your .. newly acquired .. wife."

"I have thought of that too," the Marquis admitted.

"Perhaps you could say I had drowned while bathing in

138

the sea, or that I had gone abroad to join my brother in the West Indies."

"Those are two definite possibilities," the Marquis agreed, "but you have forgotten a more obvious one."

Ivana stood looking at him in perplexity.

"What is that?" she asked.

"That your husband might object to your being married to another man!"

Again her face was suffused with colour and now she walked towards the bow-window to sit down on the window-seat looking out with what the Marquis was sure were unseeing eyes.

"Do you love him very much?" he asked unexpectedly.

"Y . yes .. yes .. of course."

"Even though he has been away for so long?"

"That is .. inevitable .. when a man is a .. sailor."

"Perhaps you were unwise in the first place to marry a man who was wedded to the sea."

Ivana drew in her breath.

"I cannot .. think that this concerns .. Your Lordship in .. any way."

"I am concerning myself with your safety," the Marquis replied. "Is your husband likely to be relegated to half-pay? In which case he will be able to be here with you."

"I .. I do not .. know."

"If you will give me his full name, his rank, the ship in which he is serving, I will talk to the First Lord of the Admiralty and find out exactly what will happen to him."

"I .. would not wish to put Your Lordship to .. so much trouble."

"It will be no trouble, and then I should no longer have to worry about you."

"There is .. no need for you to .. do that."

"There is every need. What has happened here this afternoon could easily happen again."

He saw a little shiver run through her thin body, and he went on relentlessly:

"And next time I might not be here to save you."

"Perhaps Nanny and I should . . go away once the sailors are better."

"How soon will that be?"

"In about three or four weeks."

"Anything might happen in that time."

Ivana turned to look at him.

"Please . . My Lord . . do not . . frighten me. In future I will have a loaded pistol by my bed at night . . and perhaps one in the Study . . and if Your Lordship will take the . . snuff-boxes, your watch and the . . gold ship back with you to Heathcliffe, there will be nothing valuable left in the house."

"On the contrary," the Marquis said, "there will be something of inestimable value."

He saw the question in her eyes and he said quietly:

"You!"

Their eyes met and Ivana felt it was impossible to look away.

Then after what seemed to be a long time the Marquis said:

"Now we get back to the same question – the one you have still not answered – what about your husband?"

Ivana turned her head away so that the Marquis could see only her profile silhouetted against the diamond-panes of the window.

It struck him that her features were not only as perfect as Rose's, but there was something distinctly spiritual about her whole face which could certainly not be said of any other beauty he had ever seen.

He thought too, there was something very gallant in the way she had fought with no money and little help, to assist the wounded men.

If every woman in England had the same compassion for the men who had fought against the tyranny of Bonaparte there would be far less suffering and far less dissatisfaction amongst the members of the Armed Forces.

They were silent for some minutes before the Marquis said:

"I am waiting!"

"I .. I have .. nothing to say."

"Then you have no wish for me to enquire about your husband's future?"

"You have other interests .. My Lord .. to occupy you. Forget about .. Flagstaff House."

"If you are suggesting that we should return to the battle which raged between my father and your grandfather, I can hardly think, Ivana, that you and I are likely to be adversaries on the same scale."

"I .. hope not."

"It would be far easier for us to be friends, and for you to allow me to help you."

"I thought you were .. intending to have me .. hanged!"

"Do you really believe I would have done that?"

She glanced at him and there was a shy smile on her lips.

"You .. frightened me at the .. time."

"That is what I wanted to do because I thought you deserved it. But now I am not so sure that you deserve anything, except perhaps congratulations and a medal."

Ivana's eyes seemed to light up.

"Have George and Tim made you change your mind?"

"Not George and Tim," the Marquis replied, "but a very valiant lady called Ivana!"

"Now you are teasing me, but I would like your .. reassurance that I am not to go to .. prison."

"I will leave you free."

"And you will not dismiss Marky?"

"That is a different matter altogether."

"Then if you will not let him off, I must be .. punished too. I will go to prison, or be .. hanged if that is what you prefer."

The Marquis laughed.

"Like all women you nag until you get your own way. All

right! Markham can stay but I warn you, I shall check the ledgers very carefully every month."

"Oh .. thank you .. thank you," Ivana said, clasping her hands together. "He is such a kind, generous man .. I think it would .. kill him if he had to suffer because of what he .. did for me."

"I dare say you nagged him as you have nagged me."

"That is not true," she protested, "and I hate the word 'nag'. It sounds horrid and over-bearing."

"Then I will retract it," the Marquis said, "as long as you will help me as you have helped everybody else."

"How can I do .. that?"

"I imagine the first step would be for you to accompany me to Brighton so that I can obey His Royal Highness's instructions and take you to meet Mrs. Fitzherbert."

The Marquis's lips twisted for a moment as he said:

"It is somewhat of a doubtful compliment, since those who are closest to the King and Queen, as you must be aware, will have nothing to do with her."

"I believe she is a good woman," Ivana said in a low voice, "and I am not prepared to sit in judgement upon anybody .. at the same time .. how can I .. possibly go with .. you?"

"I see no alternative," the Marquis replied. "Even if, as you suggest, you get drowned or disappear to the West Indies, people would think it strange so soon after our supposed marriage, and it would hardly be a compliment to my attractions."

"Now you are making a joke of everything," Ivana said accusingly, "and I suppose you do not really mean what you say in suggesting that I should go with you to call on Mrs. Fitzherbert."

"That I meant in all sincerity," the Marquis answered. "The Prince will undoubtedly be extremely annoyed if we leave his invitation unanswered for more than a week."

Ivana clasped her hands together.

"I .. I cannot .. do it."

"Why not?" the Marquis asked. "I have never known

anyone who can act better when it concerns her own interests. You can surely do the same for me?"

"This . . is very different."

"I should have thought it would be easier to play the part of a woman than a man."

Ivana drew in her breath.

"Please . . please do not make me . . do this . . I shall . . let you down . . I shall say all the wrong things . . and you will be ashamed . . and besides . . I have no suitable clothes in which to . . play a part like that."

As she spoke, she had a picture of Lady Rose and knew that never could she emulate anyone so smart and outstanding.

That was the sort of woman who should accompany the Marquis whether she was his wife or someone he fancied.

But for her it was utterly and completely impossible.

As if he knew exactly what she was thinking the Marquis said softly:

"The Prince thought you beautiful: 'The loveliest Marchioness of the Veryans!' Was not that what he said?"

"That is certainly not true, except . . perhaps to a . . man?"

The Marquis smiled.

"So you are afraid of what the women will think?"

"Of course!"

"That is why you want a beautiful gown in which to compete with them!"

"How do you propose I should get that?" Ivana asked sharply.

"You could always sell another snuff-box!"

She turned her face away from him again.

"Now you are mocking me."

"Shall I say I am teasing you?" the Marquis said, "If you will come to Brighton with me, I promise you shall be dressed in a fashion which will make all the other women extremely envious."

"If, by that, you are suggesting that you should buy a

gown for me, My Lord," Ivana said, "it is something I could not accept."

"It is too late to start being conventional," the Marquis objected, "after you have been so unconventional as to enter my house as though it was your own, to purloin my servants' wages, to sell a unique collection of snuff-boxes and to persuade my agent to aid and abet you!"

Ivana looked at the Marquis as he spoke and realised he was not angry as she might have expected, but under-lying everything he said was a distinct note of laughter.

"After all that," he went on, "to jib at accepting a gown, a bonnet and doubtless a pair of gloves, is not worth arguing about."

He paused for a moment before he said slowly:

"Anyway, you are no longer a young and innocent débutante who is afraid of losing her reputation, and of course, her – innocence."

He waited for the flush which suffused Ivana's face as it had done before and he thought it was very lovely, like the sun coming over the horizon.

"P . please . . My Lord . . do not make me go to Brighton," Ivana pleaded after a moment. "It would be more . . frightening than anything I have . . ever done in my life."

"I will look after you," the Marquis said. "I will see that you make no mistakes, and I promise that you will find it extremely enjoyable."

He thought Ivana was going to protest again and he said hastily:

"Before we get as far as Brighton there are other things to be done, and I am sure you realise what the first must be."

"What is that?" Ivana asked. "I have no idea."

"You must of course, come to Heathcliffe," the Marquis answered. "I have a feeling that, although we are supposed to be on our honeymoon, the news of our marriage might bring a number of guests, whether they are welcome or not, to visit me. It will seem peculiar, to say the least of it, if my wife is living in one house and I in another."

Ivana was staring at him with her eyes very wide.

"You cannot . . really mean this?"

"I certainly mean it," the Marquis replied. "First from my point of view, then from yours. And whether you are acting the part of my wife or not, I have no intention of leaving you and your Nurse alone here with five crippled men to become the prey of every scrounger who has nothing to live on but his wits."

He rose to his feet saying:

"I do not intend to argue. I am riding back now to Heathcliffe and I will order a carriage for you and your Nurse and a Landau for the injured men. Travers can arrange accommodation for them. As you know, Heathcliffe is big enough for an Army, or should I say a Navy, if necessary! Your house will be locked up, but I will see that there is someone to keep an eye on it."

As he finished speaking, the Marquis looked down at Ivana's bewildered and frightened face.

She was staring up at him, her fingers linked together in her lap like a child's and he thought how lovely she looked and at the same time very innocent and untouched.

"Leave everything to me," he said quietly.

Then as Ivana could find no words to answer him and it seemed impossible even to breathe, he went from the room and she heard his footsteps crossing the hall.

CHAPTER SEVEN

"It seems incredible that we have been here five days," Ivana said to Nanny as she was changing from her riding-habit into her green gown for tea.

"Our invalids certainly look better," Nanny replied, "and though I like to think it's the way we nurse them, I believe really, it's His Lordship's good food. I didn't, until I came here, know that so much meat existed."

Ivana smiled.

She had already heard this several times and she knew that Nanny was enjoying every moment of their visit to Heathcliffe.

She was waited on, she had plenty of other servants to talk to, and every time she was with Ivana she praised the arrangements in the household, and the manner in which everything was organised.

"I cannot imagine what Grandpapa would say if he could hear you," Ivana would say teasingly.

She knew that after years of scrimping and pinching and wondering where each penny would come from, it was, in fact, a holiday which Nanny well deserved.

For her own part she too was enjoying herself inordinately.

She had never realised how fascinating it was not only to have superb horses to ride and her every wish anticipated almost before she thought of it, but also to have all to herself the companionship of two handsome young men.

She always thought, because she had heard stories of the Marquis's extravagance and raffish behaviour, that he would

146

be stupid and uninterested in anything except the pleasures of the *Beau Monde*.

Instead she found he had read extensively and the conversation when they had meals together was so sparkling and so stimulating that she felt as if she was taking part in a play.

In fact, everything that happened at Heathcliffe seemed a theatrical fantasy and, although she would not admit it to herself, she was dreading the moment when the curtain would fall and she must go back to the life she had known before.

When she went to bed at night she found herself going over in her mind not only what had been said, but the way the Marquis had looked.

She had never imagined any man could be so amazingly handsome without apparently being conscious of it, or considering his appearance of any consequence.

It also surprised her that he was so strong, that not even the most strenuous exertions seemed to tire him.

As the weather was still very hot the Marquis and Sir Anthony swam every morning in the sea. Then they would come back glowing with health and high spirits to eat an enormous breakfast with Ivana before they all went riding.

There were great stretches of the Downs on which they could gallop until even the horses were exhausted, and there were parts of the Heathcliffe Estate which the Marquis had not seen for years and which Ivana could show him and tell him the local legends connected with them.

The two men listened to her and teased her, and Anthony paid her extravagant compliments which she laughed at as soon as she grew used to them.

She liked to think he admired her but she would wonder over and over again what the Marquis really felt about her.

It seemed to her that he watched her, but she thought he was probably being suspicious in case she did something else outrageous, or perhaps because she was different from Lady

Rose and the Beauties who had always amused him in the past.

She found herself longing as she went down to dinner in the same gown she had worn the first night she had dined at Heathcliffe, to be dressed in a manner that would make him gaze at her in admiration.

While he had remembered that the Prince of Wales had said she would be the 'loveliest Marchioness of the Veryans' he had never told her what he personally thought of her looks.

'I am sure he really admires fair-haired women like Lady Rose,' she had thought last night despairingly.

Sir Anthony had kissed her hand almost passionately as he had said good-night, but the Marquis had merely bowed in response to her curtsey, and though his eyes were on her face she had no idea what he was thinking.

Now she had the frightening feeling that the sands were running out and in two days they would be going to Brighton together as the Marquis had insisted she must.

After that there was a huge question mark over her future.

She wanted to discuss it with him again, but there had been no opportunity as Sir Anthony was always with them. But to-day might be different.

When they had turned to ride back to Heathcliffe for luncheon Anthony said unexpectedly:

"I am thinking of going to Lewes Races as soon as we get back. Are you coming with me, Justin?"

"I cannot do that," the Marquis had replied. "It would be a mistake to appear in public without Ivana and the clothes I have ordered for her from London have not yet arrived."

"Yes, in the circumstances it would be a mistake for you to be seen there," Anthony admitted, "but I will go and find out how the land lies and what people are saying about your secret marriage!"

The Marquis did not reply and Ivana looked at him nervously.

"I expect the Prince will ask when you will be bringing Ivana to see Mrs. Fitzherbert," Anthony remarked.

"Tell him it will be about the middle of next week," the Marquis replied, "and suggest tactfully if you can, that we do not want a huge crowd of fools gaping at us and would rather be alone with His Royal Highness and Mrs. Fitz."

"I doubt if he will listen to me," Anthony replied. "You know as well as I do that at the Royal Pavilion it is a case of any excuse for a party."

Ivana gave a little cry.

"Oh, please," she said, "do persuade him not to invite all his Lordship's friends! I shall be terrified anyway .. and if .."

She stopped, feeling she could not put into words what she really wanted to say, which was that, if the Marquis was occupied with other women, he would not be able to look after her.

The consternation over what might happen showed in her face, and the Marquis said quietly:

"I promise you it will not be as bad as you anticipate."

Then he started to ride faster and there was no chance of more conversation before they reached Heathcliffe.

It was the first time that Ivana had eaten a meal alone with the Marquis since she had arrived and she told herself as they walked towards the Dining-Room that she must not bore him with her fears but try to amuse him as she was certain somebody like Lady Rose would do.

Anyway it would be impossible to speak intimately with Travers and the new footmen in the room.

It did in fact, prove surprisingly easy not only to have an interesting conversation but also to make the Marquis laugh.

When after luncheon he suggested they should ride once again, this time along the shore, she had been too thrilled by the horse she was riding, and of course the Marquis, to spoil the time with him by expressing anything but her appreciation and what she knew was an inexpressible happiness.

Now as Nanny buttoned her into the familiar green gown there was a knock on the bedroom door.

Nanny went to open it, then stepped back to allow the three footmen to come in each carrying a number of boxes.

There were long ones which Ivana guessed contained gowns, and a number of round ones which were obviously made for bonnets, and others which she had no idea what they might contain.

There seemed to be dozens of them and as she gazed wide-eyed at them one of the footmen said to Nanny:

"These've just arrived from London. The coachman were sorry 'e were a bit late in bringing 'em, but th' roads were more crowded than 'e expected."

"Well, they're here now, and that's all that matters!" Nanny said.

The footmen went from the room and Ivana found her voice.

"Those .. cannot all be .. for me!"

"I hardly think as His Lordship'll be wearing a gown that comes from Bond Street!" Nanny said as she glanced at the names on the boxes.

Then as if she was too excited to wait, she started to lift the lids and unpack gowns, pelisses, night-attire, chemises and shawls, that made Ivana gasp as Nanny held them out for her inspection, one by one, before she laid them on the bed.

Never had she dreamed of seeing, let alone owning, so many fashionable and exquisite clothes each of which she was aware must have cost more than she spent in the whole year.

Finally when the bed seemed to be piled with diaphanous, exquisite, elaborate garments, Nanny turned to tackle the bonnet-boxes.

Then Ivanna gave a little cry and leaving her bedroom ran down the stairs.

She expected the Marquis would be in one of the Drawing-Rooms where they usually took tea, and as she entered the room she saw the tea-table set out with its sparkling array of silver on the hearth-rug.

The Marquis was standing at the long open window looking out into the garden.

He turned at her approach and she ran to him to say:

"How .. could you? How could .. you give me all those wonderful, exciting clothes? You know I .. cannot accept .. them."

The Marquis smiled.

"It would look very strange if as my wife, you possessed only what you are wearing now .. and I am curious to see you in the height of fashion."

"I agree that I should not .. shame you when we have to .. call on the Prince and Mrs. Fitzherbert, but what you have .. given me is .. enough for . . .."

She stopped and the Marquis finished the sentence.

".. a trousseau," he said quietly.

Ivana made a little gesture with her hands.

"You said that people might call here," she said almost accusingly," which was one .. reason for me to be well dressed .. but in the last four days .. nobody has come, and it had not .. mattered what I wore."

"You have been incorrectly informed," the Marquis replied, "for as it happens, a number of people have made an attempt to see us, but Travers on my instructions, has sent them away."

"I .. did not .. know."

"There was no reason to bother you with the information," the Marquis said, "and as I had no wish to entertain visitors they therefore had to drive back to Brighton without any tit-bits of information with which to regale those who are as curious as they are themselves."

The Marquis spoke in a contemptuous manner and Ivana said:

"I do not like to .. think that I am .. stopping you from seeing your .. friends and being with .. them."

"Shall I say I have been quite content," he asked. "But you

know as well as I do that sooner or later we shall have to be a little more sociable."

Ivana drew in her breath.

"After we have . . visited the Prince and Mrs. Fitzherbert . . I think that will be the . . moment when I should . . disappear."

Even as she spoke the words she felt as if the mere idea of disappearing was like stabbing herself with a sharp knife such as the one the sailor had produced.

Then she tried to think that she was being ridiculous and she had known all along that this would happen. The only real question was when?

"Where are you going to disappear to?" the Marquis asked.

Ivana shrugged her shoulders. Then she said:

"I have a cousin who lives in Dover. Perhaps I could stay with her for a little while."

"And that would make you happy?"

"It need not be a long visit . . and perhaps when you have . . gone away, I could come . . back to Flagstaff House."

"I thought we had already agreed that might be dangerous for you?"

"If you do not take Travers to Veryan or any of your other houses, he could keep an . . eye on us."

The Marquis did not answer and Ivana said hastily:

"Only if you would . . allow him to do so. I promise you that I will . . never again use your servants unless you . . permit it."

"Do you not think people might consider it very strange if the new Marchioness of Veryan is living in a separate house from the Marquis?"

"I had the idea that nobody need be . . aware of it," Ivana said quickly.

"You know that would be impossible."

"Then I must go . . somewhere else," she said in a low voice. "Perhaps to Scotland or Ireland . . anywhere where I would not be . . known."

She thought as she spoke it would not only be very frightening, but also the expense of the journey and having to pay for a roof over her head would be more than she could afford.

"I can only ask you the same question again," the Marquis said. "Do you think living in Scotland, Ireland or anywhere else in obscurity will make you happy?"

Ivana wanted to answer that she would be absolutely miserable, but because she was determined he should have no idea of her real feelings, she answered:

"I expect I will .. get used to it and find .. something to do."

"I think you have forgotten one very important factor in your plans for the future," the Marquis said.

There was no need for Ivana to ask him what he meant and as he glanced down at her wedding-ring, she knew that, because the Marquis had not mentioned her husband since her arrival at Heathcliffe, everything about him had slipped from her mind.

The Marquis unexpectedly reached out and took her left hand in his.

"I have a suggestion to make to you," he said, "and it is something I have been thinking about for some time."

He felt her fingers tremble in his as she asked nervously:

"What .. is it?"

He drew the wedding-ring from the third finger of her left hand.

"As this is obsolete," he said, "I would like to replace it with something more suitable."

As he spoke he drew from his pocket another ring which he put on her finger.

She was so bemused by what he was doing that she found it impossible to move or to protest, until she found herself staring down at a large and very beautiful diamond ring which glittering in the sunshine seemed almost to blind her.

"I think," the Marquis was saying quietly, "it was a very wise and sensible move on your part, considering what you were doing, to pretend to be married, but I never felt the mythical husband whose existence you kept forgetting, had any substance in fact."

"Y . you . . knew?" she whispered.

"Almost from the first," the Marquis replied, "and let me say you are not only an extremely bad liar, but you also do not look married. Even Anthony was aware of that the first time he saw you."

Ivana stood staring at the ring.

"It is . . very beautiful," she said, "but to . . convince the Prince I shall still . . need a wedding-ring."

"That I intend to give you," the Marquis said, "but not until we are actually married."

Ivana gave a little start. Then as she looked up at him, her eyes very wide, she saw that he was smiling.

"I am asking you in a rather round-about way, my darling, if you will marry me."

For a moment she was unable to breathe, then barely above a whisper she managed to murmur:

"What . . are you saying . . .? You cannot mean . . really mean . . .?"

"What I really mean," the Marquis said, "is that I am fed up with having a pretend wife, when I have discovered quite unexpectedly that more than anything else in the world, I want to be really married."

"Is that . . true . . ?"

"That is something I asked myself at first," the Marquis replied, "until I realised it was impossible to contemplate life without you."

"You are not saying that . . just because you . . feel you must . . or wish to . . deceive the Prince of Wales?"

"I am quite prepared to deceive the Prince and anybody else," the Marquis answered, "but I can no longer deceive myself. In other words, I love you! Is that what you are waiting for me to say?"

He saw the light in her eyes and the sudden radiance that swept over her face.

Then he put his arms round her and pulled her close against him and his lips found hers.

To Ivana his kiss was a miracle that swept away her fears and her apprehensions and she felt as if suddenly she had been carried into the blazing glory of the sun.

She had never been kissed before and the Marquis's lips gave her an ecstatic feeling which made her respond to him with a joy and a rapture which seemed to invade her whole body like the waves of the sea.

She did not know it was possible to feel anything so wonderful, so perfect, and as she pressed herself closer and still closer to the Marquis, she was sure that she must be dreaming.

Yet he filled the whole world and there was nothing else but the wonder of his lips and the security of his arms.

'I am safe! I am safe!' she thought, 'and I need never be .. afraid again.'

Then the Marquis was kissing her demandingly, passionately, until she was unable to breathe or even think because of the sensations he aroused in her.

The Marquis raised his head.

"My darling, my sweet," he said a little unsteadily. "I can hardly believe it true, but I believe I am the first man who has ever kissed you."

"The .. only one, and I did not .. know a kiss could be so .. wonderful!"

"Tell me what I make you feel," he asked masterfully.

"I .. love .. you. I have loved you .. ever since I first .. saw you .. but I did not know it was .. love .. until I came here to Heathcliffe."

"Then what did you feel?"

"I dreaded the .. moment when I had to .. leave and perhaps never .. see you again."

"That is something which will never happen," the Marquis said. "You are mine, Ivana, mine completely and absolutely .. and we will be together always by day – and by night."

He said the last words slowly and watched the colour flare into her cheeks. Then he pulled her close against him again.

"My darling, innocent little love," he said. "How could anyone believe for a moment you were a married woman when you blush like that?"

"I felt sure you . . . believed me," Ivana said, "even though you asked such . . embarrassing questions about . . my husband."

"The only husband you are going to have is me," the Marquis asserted, "and let me say that now you have my engagement-ring on your finger I shall not allow Anthony to go on flirting with you in that outrageous manner!"

He saw the question in her eyes and added:

"I have been jealous, crazily jealous of my best friend, very apprehensive lest you fell in love with him and there would be nothing I could do about it."

"It was you . . always . . you," Ivana said with a little throb in her voice.

She turned her face against his shoulder but the Marquis put his fingers under her chin and looked down into her eyes.

"How can I have been so lucky as to have found you?" he asked.

He would have kissed her but Ivana whispered:

"I was afraid . . terribly afraid that you would change your mind . . and would want . . after all to marry . . the beautiful Lady Rose."

"That I have never wanted to do," the Marquis said positively, "and, my darling, in case you are worrying about her, I promise you there will be no more Rose's or women of her sort in my life. I know now that what I was seeking undoubtedly in all the wrong places – was you."

"I will try to be . . everything you want me to be," Ivana said humbly, "and do exactly what you . . wish."

The Marquis laughed.

"I very much doubt it," he said, "and I think because you

are so original, and have so much personality, my lovely one, you will intrigue, delight and even mystify me, however many years we are together."

He put his lips against the softness of her cheek before he said:

"How could I have imagined in my wildest dreams that I would marry a Highwayman?"

His arms tightened as he added:

"You looked very elegant in your breeches, but they are something you will never wear again for any man to see, except myself."

"You sound as if I . . shocked you."

"I was shocked that I should be held up by a woman, but I am much more shocked now I know, that it was someone adorable and very alluring who is to be my wife."

Ivana gave a little sigh of sheer happiness. Then she said:

"It is not really . . right for you to marry . . anyone like me. Supposing you are . . disappointed when you see me among your . . friends and are able to compare me with great Beauties who . . I am sure . . love you as I do?"

There was a deep tenderness in the Marquis's eyes as he looked down at Ivana's worried blue ones before he answered:

"I think the love that you and I have for each other, my precious one, is very different from the love that is talked about so lightly in the Fashionable World."

"The love I have for you," she said very softly, "is sacred and part of God. I love you until you fill the whole world and the sky! The only thing I want and pray for is that I shall make you . . happy."

The Marquis held her so tightly that she could hardly breathe.

"That is the love I have been looking for," he said, "and that is the love I thought I should never find."

He kissed both her dimples before he added:

"I am the most fortunate man in the world, and just as you want to make me happy, my sweet darling, I want to give you the sun, the moon and the stars and a love that is greater than any woman has ever received before."

"How can you say such . . wonderful things to me?" Ivana asked. 'First you frightened me . . then when I loved you, I thought you were so far out of . . reach that apart from the fact that we were . . involved together in a . . pretended marriage I would never be really close to you, like . . this."

"You will be closer still," the Marquis said, "but I think we should get properly married first."

He smiled very tenderly, as he saw Ivana blush again. Then he said:

"I will send Markham to Canterbury for a Special Licence. Then, my Sweetheart, we will be married very quietly early in the morning in the village Church with only Anthony as a witness. Will that please you?"

"I think . . because it is so . . marvellous," Ivana said, "I am going to . . cry."

"You did not cry when you were threatened with a knife," the Marquis said. "You did not cry when I told you you might be hanged. If you cry now, I shall feel I have failed to give you the happiness that you have given me."

Ivana blinked the tears away from her eyes.

She looked so lovely as she did so, that the Marquis moved his lips first over the softness of her cheeks, then lower to the rounded column of her neck.

Ivana felt a strange thrill run through her body like quick-silver and her lips parted.

"Please . . please . . ." she whispered.

The Marquis raised her head.

"Do you not like my kissing you like that, my darling?"

"I like it . . but it . . makes me . . feel so . . excited . . and . . wild!"

He smiled.

"That is how I want you to feel . . I have so much to teach you, my dearest Heart."

She moved a little closer to him.

"Teach me . . please teach me."

He looked down at her with a tenderness that no woman had ever seen before.

"I worship you," he said softly.

"And I love .. you .. I love .. you!" Ivana said with a touch of passion which made the Marquis seek her lips.

He kissed her until the room seemed to spin dizzily around them both and once again Ivana felt he carried her into the blazing light of the sun, and they were one with the burning glory of it.

Then the Marquis set her lips free and it was as if she broke under the very strain of it Ivana made an incoherent little murmur and hid her face against his shoulder.

She was conscious as she did so, that his heart was beating as violently as hers, and she thrilled to know that she could arouse and excite him.

Because he was human as well as divine, it made her feel even closer to him than she was already.

"You are so .. magnificent!" she exclaimed.

"And you are so soft, sweet as well as beautiful that I have no words with which to tell you how much I want to kiss you from the top of your head to the soles of your little feet."

He spoke with a deep, passionate note in his voice and Ivana whispered:

"You .. make me feel .. shy."

"I adore you when you look shy," the Marquis replied. "I had forgotten there were women in the world who could blush and your shyness, my precious one, thrills me in a way nothing has ever done before."

His lips moved across her forehead before he said:

"Look at me."

She raised her head and his eyes searched her face before he said hoarsely:

"I want you .. I want you now, this moment and for all eternity."

The words seemed to come from the very depths of his being, then as if he tried to speak more calmly, he said:

"I suppose I should really be taking you to task, my lovely one, for stealing from me one more of my possessions."

"Stealing?" Ivana questioned.

"You have stolen my heart. It is something which I thought was safe from the most determined and experienced of robbers, and now I have lost it. It is in your keeping for all time."

"I will never .. let it go," Ivana cried, "I shall love it .. cherish it .. adore it, and as long as I can keep it, I want nothing else in the .. whole world."

The last words were swept away by the Marquis's lips.

Then as he kissed her fiercely, demandingly, possessively, Ivana knew they had found that which all people seek, the perfect love that can never, in fact, be stolen, but only given by God.

THE END